A footstep. A voice. The deadly click of a silenced gun. Rich gay art dealer Alex Horvay lies dead on the floor of a Brooklyn warehouse.

Even in New York City, this is a class-A case. For Detective Inspector Lenny Schwartz, it's A-plus, his chance to make up for taking the cocaine bribe that is putting his son through Yale.

So he goes for it. Through the fog of a cover-up masterminded in a high place, Lenny Schwartz realizes that this is no mere murder investigation but an epic psychological duel with a brilliant killer.

TAILOR'S DUMMY

"An exciting debut . . . one looks forward to the additional adventures of Lieutenant Lenny Schwartz."
Newgate Callendar,
The New York Times Book Review

TAILOR'S DUMMY

Irving Weinman

FAWCETT CREST • NEW YORK

A Fawcett Crest Book
Published by Ballantine Books
Copyright © 1986 by Irving Weinman

Library of Congress Catalog Card Number: 85-47775

ISBN 0-449-21201-7

This edition published by arrangement with Atheneum Publishers,
a division of The Scribner Book Companies, Inc.

Manufactured in the United States of America

First Ballantine Books Edition: August 1987

To E.L. FOR LOCKING ME INTO THE WRITING ROOM.
To J.K. FOR FINDING THE KEY.

BOOK I

1

He was six foot four and had light brown wavy hair, a straight nose and large blue eyes flecked with green. Not the kind of looks that many men would remember, but women found him attractive. They caught themselves looking and looking. Most times what they saw were bright, quick eyes that registered and then fixed, pleasantly enough, on something that wasn't there. Sometimes a woman would seem to see the eyes change color, go lighter and narrow and hard, and she'd look away, unsure.

But no one would have looked close today. It was a bright winter morning so cold, with such a wind cutting down the East River and slicing into Brooklyn, that people went about their business—milk, rolls, the Sunday papers—with heads down, buried in scarves.

Washington Street heading down into Wallabout was

nearly lifeless. Only his tall figure, and behind a chain playground fence three black boys played basketball, rubbing their hands between shots.

He checked his watch. Still plenty of time. The area was almost deserted and he wasn't really conspicuous: enough well-dressed white businessmen showed up here—lawyers, realtors, the grafters of Brooklyn politics. There were a lot of deals to be made in and around the old navy yard.

He crossed under the Brooklyn-Queens Expressway. It smelled of rubber, grease and oil: a car sewer for the road above. A piece of blue-black river shone down there, past empty factories. The cold January sun. Block after block of broken windows that had thrived, boomed and dropped dead with the navy yard.

Behind the camel-hair collar and black cashmere scarf, he smiled in his own warm breath. The small thoughts were fine with him, meant he was relaxed. Slowing and looking up, he turned into the alley between two factories and followed it around to a yard in back. He went up the rusting iron stairs onto a loading platform and pushed open the low wooden door. It smelled worse than under the expressway. Dust and cat piss brought his hand to his nose as he went up the flight of wooden stairs to the second floor. Less of a smell here, a big space, fifteen thousand or so square feet across a glade of iron columns rusting through blue paint. They cast long diagonal shadows in the sunlight.

Ten minutes later a cream-colored Mercedes coupé came down the street, passed the alleyway, backed up to it, turned in and parked by the loading platform. A short, plump man in a fur hat and fur-collared brown leather coat got out. He looked at the building for a few seconds, then went up the platform stairs and through the low door. On the second floor he looked at his watch.

"Parker, you here?" he asked.

Before his echo died, the gun with its silencer made the sound of a small hammer hitting a small nail.

The man looked at the figure on its back. Something about the clothing made him come closer. The trousers, that tweed.

"Oh. Him. Four thousand dollars of clothes, and it still looks like Salvation Army."

He put the gun away and left.

2

It was a small bribe, as cocaine bribes go. Seventy-five thousand dollars. And it wasn't going well. They talked about it, they talked about it, and afterwards Schwartz would go on talking about it to himself, though he knew it would lead nowhere except to a sour stomach, which kept Karen awake.

Then it would be three in the morning, and they'd make tea in the kitchen and talk some more until Schwartz decided the hell with it and they'd go back to bed. But still no sleep because first a tremendous tenderness for Karen, and he'd spoon his body to hers and try to sleep. But then they couldn't sleep because she'd feel him growing excited and she'd get excited, and finally they'd make love. And lately he'd found himself crying when he came, calling out, "Karen, Karen," big tears falling slowly, incredibly from his eyes.

So by the time they got to sleep it could be four in the morning, and they'd be up at seven, exhausted, nervous, touching each other as they washed, dressed, had breakfast.

Karen was writing up notes at home, so Schwartz drove in from Park Slope to Manhattan on his own. No sooner had he nosed the car into the Flatbush Avenue traffic than he started going over all of it again, looking for some order.

Why, for starters, had Leonard Schwartz, nice Jewish boy, become a cop? Magna at Harvard yet, he could have been anything, y'know? Doctor, lawyer, stockbroker, professor, doctor, anything, and didn't even finish his doctorate at Chicago, in sociology, y'know?

Schwartz pursed his lips, hearing the argument in the stereotyped voice. Nobody in his family actually spoke that way, but that was their thinking. So why quit and join the police, the police yet, in the sixties?

Well, that was the good thing then, getting into real life, away from the petrified forest of academe.

Up ahead, Schwartz saw lights flashing before the Manhattan Bridge. Breakdown, accident. Wonderful! And him in his own car, no siren.

Sure it was reaction against family expectations. And really radical, a sixties radical joining the world, the involvement with real lives. Sure. And yes, yes, all that about the cop's attraction to the criminal, the criminal in the cop. And then there was his old arrogance, thinking that the cops could use a "better" sort, like him. But that had stopped years ago. He hoped.

He said to himself, Look, Len, you took it, took the bribe to look the other way. Like all the other cops that had. And at what cost? Another few keys of coke up the noses of bankers' kids? Or up the bankers' noses? Big deal, with the blizzards of the stuff falling on New York.

What rationalizing. Maybe he just couldn't live with it as comfortably as others. They didn't catch him. The investigation showed nothing. But of course, they knew.

Cars were blowing their horns. Oh, that would certainly solve the jam. Where were the cops when . . . Yeah, and when he'd needed them, especially his famous partner, Gallagher. Ex-partner. They didn't have anything on Schwartz, but they'd frozen him out. Five years of cold war, fewer and fewer real cases. They were making him a teacher, a goddamned PR man for the department.

Nice bind, caught between an anti-Semitism which liked to see him fall and a pro-Semitism, just as bad, which thought it worse for him, a Jew, to fall.

First he'd been his precinct's token liberal. The crap he'd taken. But he'd been right, fewer heads were broken now, and now the force had more and better blacks, Hispanics. But so many still were racist scum. Tom Gallagher.

"Shut the hell up," Schwartz said behind the steamed side window at a trailer truck honking away.

Yet Gallagher, who despised him, had taken two bullets in his lungs to save Schwartz's life, had pain from them yet. Jesus, and Gallagher's Jersey house and Long Island summer house—what cop's salary were those from? No, Gallagher was a clever politician. And the politics dripped down from the top, the last five years less caring, crueler, the sixties and seventies progress eroding. Tighter budgets, tighter laws, attitudes, sentencing. But that's what he had to stick around to fight, wasn't it?

Shit! The car behind had bumped him. Not hard. Maybe a dent, maybe not. The hell with getting out in this cold to watch the driver's face drop when he flashed his badge. He looked in the rearview mirror. The driver, an old Latino in a baseball hat and earmuffs, was making "sorry" signs.

His good deed for the day. Like putting the bribe money into Jake's college education. Come on, Leonard, cut the crap. You did wrong. You were the department's fall guy that season. But you were too fucking clever and you made them look bad and they knew it and so they got you for it in their own time-honored ways. Freeze. Freeze, like the weather.

Clever. Even the IRS found nothing. Yeah, and still, there were other detective inspectors with five times his money and not by virtue of their boyish, Celtic charms. He was second-in-command of nothing. Whoever was keeping him there was way over his head, over Gallagher's, too, he'd bet. He'd stop thinking of it.

Ten minutes later, on the bridge, Schwartz thought about it, about how it was getting to him, about how, maybe, it was getting to him now because of his newly, sensationally successful wife. No, he wasn't that mean a prick. But Jesus, if he could only really work again. He'd even work with Gallagher. The old team: Abbott and Costello, Gallagher and Sheenie.

Here were those buildings again, those buildings. Tombs, Police Plaza. He pulled into his parking space and trotted from the car to the door, the air freezing in his throat. Still the energy, excitement coming in, but by the time he reached his office they'd gone.

"Morning, Bob," Schwartz said in as friendly and informal a way as he could.

It never worked. Malinowski looked startled, pushed the typewriter away and leaped up, hitting his big knees under the desk.

"Good morning, sir! Oh. I'm sorry. I know you don't like me calling you sir, but—"

"All right, Bob, all right. Any messages?" asked Schwartz, thinking that Bob was a hard-working young man with the intelligence of a steam iron.

"Yes, sir. Sorry. Yes, one came in from the chief's office. They'd like you to respond right away."

"Fine, thanks," Schwartz said over his shoulder. Actually Bob was very clever in his own way, a desk detective, a computer freak. It was his hero worship that was hard to take, that's all.

Schwartz shut the inner office door. "Immediate response." Sure, probably another big deal like a community board meeting or the Bowery Commission, et cetera, ad nauseam. He unfolded the message sheet.

"Jesus," he said aloud, "think of the devil."

3

Tom Gallagher sat with his big hands folded on his desk. He moved to get up when Schwartz came in, but he changed his mind and sat back.

"Hello, Lenny. Jeez, you're in good shape. Playing a lot of squash, are you?"

"Squash, weights, running. I've got lots of free time, Tom. You look . . . very successful, very deputy chief of detectives."

"Sure. Could've been you, too, if you kept your nose clean."

"You mean, if the big boys hadn't decided to look in my Kleenex when I blew it."

"We're all big boys now." Gallagher pushed away from the desk and turned his chair towards the window. "Maybe it's that big Jewish nose of yours."

"So are we here to discuss my nose and how much more professionally some of us can take bribes?"

"Ha!" Gallagher snorted, turning back. "Always the same tough guy. No, Lenny, something's come up I want you in on. A murder in Brooklyn ten days ago."

"Why isn't Brooklyn handling it?"

"Doesn't belong in Brooklyn. This was a big shot art gallery type, very professionally killed. Looks like a contract—over in an empty factory behind the navy yard. Patrol saw his Mercedes parked, checked, found him frozen stiff upstairs. No struggle, no nothing."

"Had to be a setup. But why me? Why all of a sudden me?" Schwartz asked, feeling his face go tight.

"Want me to tell you I thought it's about time you got a break? I won't. You've been locked out long enough so you're safe to use, and I want you 'cause you're good and because—as you always point out—I'm one ambitious Irishman. That enough?"

"Sure. You know I'll jump at anything to get real work again." Schwartz put his hands on the folder. "This?"

Gallagher nodded and placed his hand on the other side. "Let's just get it clear from the start that you're working with me and for me and my unit on this one. Cooperation. No waves. Right?"

"Of course, Tom. The team's the thing. Uh, by the way, you wouldn't be setting me up, would you?"

"No! What the hell! Look, I get a small, strange case thrown my way here. Nothing major. So I figure I can use you, and it's your sort of thing—art world and all that culture crap. And that's it."

"OK, Tom. 'Culture crap.' How can I resist your gift for the gab?"

Gallagher stood up with a big smile. He was six-two, and the pin-stripe suit couldn't hide his beer-barrel build. Schwartz, dark, wiry and half a foot shorter, took the file, shaking the hand his ex-partner, new boss, offered.

"Lenny, it's good to be working with you again. For what it's worth, looks like Horvay, the victim, was a raving faggot. I figure it's one of *those* murders."

Schwartz shook his head. "Tom, I'm impressed. Five years ago you wouldn't have wanted the case; it would have been in your 'one less faggot' category. Who knows, in another five you might even be calling them gay."

"Maybe, maybe not. But for sure you'll still be the same Ivy League bleeding heart."

"As well as a smart-ass."

"Goes without saying. Hey, give my best to Karen. She all right?"

"Fine, fine."

As Schwartz went towards the door, the name connected. Horvay, the Alex Horvay Gallery. Well, Gallagher could be right, but there was at least one other factor involved—big money.

4

Gerald Vandevelde, chairman of the Department of European Painting, went to the window. Out below, the grass in Central Park was brittle white in the freezing afternoon. Remnants of old snow lay in low heaps crusted with gray-black soot. He turned back towards the small office. Much nicer to look at the boule writing desk, his own, and the Dutch landscape, the museum's, purchased on his recommendation. He went to work on the catalog notes.

At four he spent fifteen minutes with Georgia Morris, the department's administrator. Then he left the museum and headed west into the park. He stopped by the first foot-tunnel entrance, turned his collar up and paced back and forth on the icy gravel. A man in a green track suit jogged into the far end of the tunnel. Vandevelde walked in to the middle, where the

14

jogger stood running in place, handed him a small package, smiled, patted his green shoulder encouragingly and walked out, off towards Fifth Avenue.

Twenty-five minutes later there was almost no daylight left in the park. A white mist hung over the frozen model sailboat pond as the man in green jogged around it. He kept looking, turning his head. No one else was there. He was sweating, steaming. His heart pounded in his eardrums.

He passed the Hans Christian Andersen statue, its nose rubbed shiny from the hands of children. Something tapped his shoulder and he stumbled. His heart beat wildly.

"Oh, it's you. Thank God! I was sure I was going to be mugged. Here, for heaven's sake, take it," he said, handing the package to the tall man in the camel-hair coat.

The man slipped it into his pocket.

"Don't you want to check?"

"No," the man said, "it's all right. I know it is." Then he smiled. "But are you all right?"

They stood next to the bronze Ugly Duckling.

"I'm much better now," he answered, beginning to run in place against the cold. "That's it then?"

"Yes. Oh, just," said the man, putting his arm around the jogger's shoulder, "this."

At that moment Gerald Vandevelde was at his tailors, Hervey and Hervey, on Madison, swatches of tweed in his hand. He was laughing at something being said to him by Bill Farley, former governor of New York.

5

As usual, Schwartz didn't keep Karen out of it. But this time he was direct; as an art historian she could help him.

"What do you know about the Alex Horvay Gallery?"

She looked up from her book, and Schwartz knew Karen knew what it was all about. The game they played was that of course, she wouldn't ask why he wanted to know.

"Horvay," she said. "Very big, very smooth. Old masters, most seventeenth- and eighteenth-century Dutch, some French. Not Hals or Poussin, well, maybe a Poussin once, but I think mostly the best of the second best—Dou, Cuyp, Hobbema, De Wit, like that."

"So they're not really so valuable?"

"Are you kidding?" Karen laughed and put down her book. "It's not my period, but I know those prices have to be, at the least, at the bottom end, oh, half a million."

"Aha, big, big bucks. Hm. What's Horvay's reputation?"

"First-class, very reputable, as far as I know. I could ask around . . ." she said, making it something between a statement and question, giving Schwartz room. He didn't respond.

"Have you seen it in the paper, about Horvay's murder?"

"Yes. Are you . . ."

"Yeah, they've given it to me—under dear old Tom Gallagher. But it's something."

"Something?" Karen moved across the sofa and hugged him. "Oh, Len, Len, they're letting you in again, don't you see? It's terrific. This is what you've been wanting for so long."

Her excitement caught him, for a bit. "Well, yeah, I am pleased. On the other hand, there's Gallagher to contend with. And some funny feeling I have about this case."

"What's that?"

"Nothing I can figure. On the face of it the most likely lead is just what Tom thinks: Horvay was gay, went in for very rough trade."

"Are you chasing it?"

"No. I should, and I'm going to have to. But I'm putting it off. I'm trying to start some other way. Maybe I just don't want to poke around all that West Side sleaze."

"Why not assign a gay detective?" Karen asked.

"Ho, Jesus. We're more liberal than, I don't know,

Dallas, and of course, we must have detectives who are gay; but they're not going to step forward and stop their careers like that. A good idea, but we're not quite ready for it."

"Maybe us liberal *shiksas* are more liberal than you liberal Jews. You should hire more of us."

"As far as I'm concerned, liberal *shiksas* should run my office, become chief of detectives, police commissioner; they should replace Crazy Eddie as mayor."

She smiled at him. Then she said, "Len, let's make love. Let's get into bed now, not wait for the middle of the night."

And he felt different; even watching her undress in their bedroom was different, more relaxed, slower, better than for months. It was as if he'd forgotten how beautiful her breasts were, the smoothness of her skin and how he loved the smell of her. And afterwards, before they fell asleep, she said, "This is the first time in months you haven't cried. You'll sleep well."

He didn't. He woke up in the middle of the night yelling, "Laundry!" His yelling woke Karen.

"Tell me," she said, her arms behind his head, across his hard black-haired chest.

"I was sitting in the backyard with three other guys. One of them, a sort of idiot, offered cocaine, threw out mounds of it in front of us and told us it was all right because he'd been to a party and they'd given him a big bag of it. Then he wetted it down with the hose, started making a clay paste of it, smearing it everywhere. Then two guys appeared from behind a hedge. One of them was laughing and drunk and flashed his wallet, but I knew he was no cop. I got scared. I knew these two guys owned the coke and would kill us for it." Schwartz stopped and licked his dry lips.

"So then we started picking it up and putting it into this big plastic garbage bag. And they took us into a garage at some house, where we kept taking the coke out of our pockets and dusting it off our clothes and putting it into the plastic bag. Then the two guys went into another room, and one came back and told us they'd send us home after they gave us one final search for more cocaine. And we had to go into that room one at a time." He stopped again, breathing as if he were winded.

"Shh. Relax, darling. Breathe deeply," Karen said softly.

"I knew they'd kill us in there. The others went first. I could hear the gunshots. The three others were dead. The guy came for me. As we went into that room, I told him that I had more coke, and he let me reach into my pocket for it. I pulled my gun, pulled him to me and shot him in the back of the head, using him for a shield against the other guy, who shot at me but hit him. Then I shot the other guy in the arm, and he fell. Then I killed him and emptied out a big box of detergent and put the coke bag in it and put some blue detergent on top of it and ran out of that house and down to a launderette, where I pretended to be washing the clothes of the three other dead guys. But they—some people—came for me anyway. And that's when I woke and started to scream. Strange. I mean, not the dream so much as getting so scared."

Karen held Schwartz tighter. "The dream is bad

enough. For anyone but a cop, I guess. You're all right now. Go to sleep."

It seemed that he'd just shut his eyes when the phone rang.

"Schwartz. . . . Yes. This is Inspector Schwartz. . . . What? This better be good. . . . What? . . . OK. What time is it? . . . OK. I'll be there in fifteen or twenty minutes."

"What is it?" Karen moaned, half asleep.

"Nothing. I have to go. Go back to sleep."

It was five-thirty in the morning. Detective Inspector Schwartz had just been informed, on the authority of Deputy Chief of Detectives Gallagher's office, that a jogger had been murdered in Central Park. He'd been found sitting on the lap of Hans Christian Andersen. They thought he might be interested.

6

They left him there for Schwartz to see. The frozen corpse in green sat as if being read to.

"Some bedtime story," he said to Bob, who was there with coffee and "good morning, sir" as if it were ten o'clock in a warm office rather than a quarter to six with breath burning the throat in the white, freezing fog.

While the photos were taken, he went over to Santini, the thin, sallow and excellent department forensics specialist.

"Hi, Gerry. What's our best doctor doing before office hours?"

"Whadya say, hotshot? My turn for house calls."

"Well, what's the diagnosis?" Schwartz asked, walking away from the police crowd around the statue.

"Can't say until I get a real look, but did you see

the dark blue at the top of the nose and under the eyes?"

"No, I didn't look that close. I just took in the whole sick picture."

"It looks like the nose bone may have penetrated the brain."

"Hmm. Nasty." Schwartz thought. "You mean, killed by putting two fingers up the nostrils from behind and pulling back hard and fast?"

"Well, it could be. I'll let you know more by midmorning. Give you any ideas, Lenny?"

"It's a military technique. Could be ex-army, ranger, Green Beret type, but not necessarily. Very practiced, though, very professional."

They turned and walked back along the path. Something about the morning began to worry Schwartz. He looked at the patrolmen cordoning off the area. The body was being taken away.

"How's the beautiful Karen?"

"Fine. In bed, where I'd like to be," Schwartz said, his mind still searching for the right question.

"Me, too," said Santini. "I mean—" He started to laugh.

"You must have some bedside manner, Gerry."

"So they say. Not that it matters on this job. Hey, I'll get you later."

Bob was coming towards him, shy and deferential. Yes, Schwartz started thinking, nodding to no one in particular. Bob nodded back. Yes, damn it. He'd been sleepwalking! Why was he called here? What did Gallagher know to link this with the Horvay murder? And Gerry Santini—he'd been on the Horvay case, too—another coincidence? Now he was sure. Everything he did was being watched for Gallagher. By Bob? No. But Gallagher was keeping tabs. Because the department still didn't trust him? Or was it Schwartz, the work-hungry patsy, being set up for some big fall? But he couldn't confront Gallagher. Not yet.

He'd have to do some hunting on his own.

7

There was something John Sheridan had to remember. There was the ten o'clock appointment at Hervey and Hervey's, but it wasn't that. Well, it would come. It was a fine suit, a lightweight wool in gray that he was having made for spring.

He'd been going to Hervey and Hervey's for years. They were the best tailors in America. Anywhere. He'd once been in England long enough to have a suit made at Huntsman's. He'd hated it: too tight-waisted and too flared out over his butt like a skirt. He'd never worn it, come back to New York and given it away to a Salvation Army store. It amused him to think of someone buying it for twenty dollars and thinking it might be worth a bit more.

It was nine, and Sheridan was nearing the end of his two-hour morning workout. He didn't like health clubs—they weren't real gyms; they were for fat-assed housewives and potbellied businessmen. But this one, at least, had real weights in addition to those stupid machines. And it was close to his apartment. Other things he could do at home. Still others were farther off—the gun club in Greenwich Village and Sejeki Niko in Tribeca for his martial arts.

He ended the workout with bench presses, pushing up, up, always going for one more than he could do, feeling the good pain, the total commitment. He let the weights fall on the rack, stretched his arms back and breathed deeply. Air moved through the loose gray sweat shirt and sweat pants, cooling him. He wasn't musclebound; he despised the body builders, inept athletes, all of them. But his loose sweat suits covered a body that would otherwise be too noticeable in a place like this, would lead to too many assumptions, questions. Not that many came in here for real weights. The few that did were generally put off chattering by the pace and seriousness of his workout. And when some did occasionally ask about weights or exercises, he'd answer politely but quickly and with a chill finality that shut them up.

He showered, dressed and left the health club, nodding with pleasant uninterest at the T-shirted woman at the desk, who always shifted on her seat when she said, "Bye-bye, Mr. S."

He walked the fifteen blocks up Madison. What was it? After the tailors he'd work at the computer analyzing the investment options for the three hundred thousand dollars. No, that wasn't it.

He stopped for coffee and fruit at a restaurant. Just forget and it will come, he told himself.

Twenty minutes later the elevator doors opened onto the fifth floor. Sheridan crossed the corridor and pushed the button by the small brass plate. The door opened to the familiar room with its long mahogany sample tables, shelves of fine material, old chairs, smell of new wool and old leather.

"Good morning, Charles. How are you?"

"Fine, sir. And how are you, Mr. Sheridan?"

"Fine," said Sheridan. And then he remembered. Yes, perhaps he'd better in this instance. It might be amusing finding out who'd hired him to kill old Alex Horvay.

―――――― **8**

Away from the offices, files, computer printouts, green data on VDUs, "yes, Inspector," "no, Inspector" and "we'll see what we can do, Inspector," Schwartz felt better. Certain things were better done alone, low-key, low-profile. That's how he and Gallagher had worked, the pair of them; only Gallagher had also known how to play the unit concept, that old "team" bullshit, which really came down to promotion credit for the team leaders. He'd moved with Gallagher up to inspector that way. Gallagher kept moving—deputy chief now, who knows what later?

Anyway, he thought, parking the car a few days later at a hydrant on Twelfth Street, it's time to do it my way. Maybe the case would start moving. He went into the bookstore and asked to see Ed Ginsberg. He didn't say "police"; he said, "Tell him Len Schwartz."

They'd been friends since Harvard. Half his books had come from the stores Ed had worked in, managed and now this one he owned.

"Hey, Len." Ed's bald head shone out from his office door. "Come in. Phil, get us two coffees, black, no sugar. Thanks."

"Hi, Ed. Jesus, you're still tanned from your holiday."

Ed clapped a hand on his head. "Vat you make fun my baldness of for? So? What's doing? Want Ruskin? You or Karen want a first edition of *Stones of Venice?*"

"No. We've got a second. You sold it to us."

"Well, you know, it's like cars, only backwards. I'll take the later model as a trade-in on the earlier."

"No, thanks. I'm just a poor cop, and Karen's book was a critical success. You know what *critical* success means?"

"Sure. No first of Ruskin. So what do you want? A Georgette Heyer used paperback? Some remaindered low-cholesterol cookbook? You want me to buy you lunch? It's not time. Fix a parking ticket? Solve a crime? What, what?"

"Yeah, well, solve a crime would be good. I want your sociological advice. Did you happen to know someone named Alex Horvay?"

"No. Oh, the art dealer who was murdered. No. Oh-oh, I get it. Was he gay? Sure. And I'm your tame gay buddy. And all us gays know each other, right? All half million or more of us in New York get down together in that big, oily bath each weekend exchanging gossip and bacteria. Right? Wrong." Ed paused, red-faced, then let out a long breath. "Wrong of me, too, Len. Sorry. It's a reflex action. Understand? *Capice, camerata?"*

Schwartz nodded, thinking of Ed and Ben together for ten years now, of Ed at thirty telling his Orthodox parents, "It's all right, Mom, Dad, he's Jewish." And then Schwartz said, "I'm sorry, too. No, I wanted to ask you—a guy who went in for rough trade, where would he hang out?"

"A guy like Horvay with a lot of money? I guess he could hang out anywhere or nowhere. I mean, he could have it delivered, like a corned beef sandwich with mustard, by calling the deli. On the other hand, he might like the thrill of the chase, the place, the punch in the face. So maybe Christopher Street, or a rough place like the Ramrod, or . . . I hear such horror stories they'd drive you celibate about the Stick Em Up Club. Charming name, no? Outside, the sign has a gun provocatively pointed at a cowboy with his hands up. Inside, supposedly, it's two fists, definitely rampant, not couchant, as they say. Yuk. So what do you think?"

"I think thanks. Thanks for being helpful and not taking a swipe at me. Listen, we'll give you a call tonight and set up dinner with you and Ben for next week or so at our place. My entrée, Karen's hors d'oeuvres."

"Wonderful, Len. Sorry I got mad. Wasn't at you. Best to Karen. Say, what about Cézanne's letters?"

"Haven't heard from him in months. No. Karen has them. Bought the book from you."

"No. I knew she had it, but not from me. Just

testing. Bye. I'm still looking out for that early Chicago school stuff for you."

"Take care, Ed." Schwartz hugged Ed and left, just as the assistant came through with the coffees.

"Nice timing, boychik," Ed said, laughing.

In the car Schwartz looked at a notebook and drove west across the Village onto Greenwich Street, then up to the Gansevoort meat market. A few blocks to the north the rough gay clubs began. They looked like nothing in the daytime or, from the outside, at night. Except he'd seen them at night, knew the muggings and beatings and some murders. All low priority for New York's Finest, unless someone of real clout was involved. He saw the crudely painted sign and parked the car.

He rang the bell on a black garage door. A panel the size of a hand slid open. The face behind said, "What?" in a high, piping voice.

"This," said Schwartz, putting the badge wallet up to the panel.

The voice squealed, "What shit is this? We're all paid up—our taxes, our license, our bribes to cops."

"Yeah, yeah, I'm sure. Something else, some questions, right now. 'Cause if you're such an efficient business, the boss should be here counting his money."

The panel shut and a small door opened in.

"Money, my red rectum. I own the place, and I'm trying to figure out how much my bartenders robbed me last night. Come on in." High voice, the figure back in the shadows.

Schwartz wasn't tall, five-eight, but he had to bend low through the little door. He kept his right hand on the butt of his gun as he went through. But there was no trouble. In the dim light he stood in what at night would be the main entrance, behind the garage door. And there was the other sign, as crude as Ed had thought. But far more detailed.

"Whoa," Schwartz said involuntarily.

"Don't know the meaning of that word here, pardner," said the mincing voice, stepping from the shadow. "I'm Cal. This way."

Cal was a foot taller than Schwartz and maybe a hundred pounds heavier. The hundred pounds was all muscle, scar and permanent smirk.

9

Cal had ducked under the long chrome bar. It was hard for Schwartz to believe the voice could come from that body.

"*Quelque chose* to drink?"

Schwartz shook his head. Above the bottles, in metal frames, photo after photo of a naked giant, with an erection to match. Cal. Schwartz looked down, scowling.

"Ah, I see. Not your affectional preference. Well, that's OK. Live and let live, say I."

"Do you?" Schwartz pulled the photosheet from his pocket and put it on the bar. "What about him? Someone didn't let him live. Know him? His name was Alex Horvay."

"Didn't know his name, I mean that name. Close, though. Here he was Alice Hooray. Cute, when you think of it. So what can I tell you?" Cal poured a

Perrier and sipped it with his little finger up. The little finger had two steel rings above and below its bottom joint. They were joined by little chains.

"You can tell me everything, starting with why you haven't come to the police. You must have seen the papers. The news must trickle down even to here."

"First of all, sweets, I do not read the papers. Second, sure there's been talk of it, but third or wherever the hell I was, I have enough woe from you people without traipsing in—I mean, me, I mean, do you expect *me* to swan in to my local gendarmerie and say I *knew* the dear deceased? I'm kinky, darling, but not *complètement fou!*"

"All right. So Alex, Alice, whatever, did he come here often? And who did he go with? Now there's two questions at once. I think you can handle it, and I'm not a paying customer, so spare me the floor show."

"Ooh. Yes, sir," Cal piped. "He was a regular enough customer. Sometimes five nights running, then once or twice a week, then nightly again. Like that. Well, as the mayor says, how'm I doing?"

"Better. Go on."

"Good. I do so like to please. Well, who'd he go with? That's easy and hard. Like me, dearest. Oops, sorry. I mean, he was what we call promiscuous. Went with one and all. Actually he was something of a fucking machine. Never had him myself, though he made some passes."

"He go with rough types particularly?"

"Rough types? Officer, Officer, look around, darling. This isn't exactly the Café Carlyle, is it? We're all rough boys and girls in here. And though you may find this *très difficile* to understand, I don't check whether my customers are in the Social Register or Hell's Angels or are butchers or even cops. OK?"

"Sure." Schwartz got off the barstool, took out the photosheet on Parker, the murdered jogger, and put it on the bar.

"Now, Mr. Anderson," he said in a low, steady voice, looking up at Cal, "there are the photos of two murdered men. One of them you admit knowing. But you'll have to do better. Tonight some police detectives will visit you—probably when you're busiest. What they'll want is names and any other identification on Horvay's 'companions.' And the same, if you could, on the other person. George Parker was his name. And they'll be back tomorrow night, too. And then, if I feel you haven't been fully cooperative, I'll pull you in. More, Mr. Anderson. I'll have so steady a stream of fire, health and building inspectors in here, not to mention drug and vice squads, that you'll be very lucky to do business here one day out of each month."

Schwartz walked off, then turned. "Have I made myself clear, Mr. Anderson?"

Cal's face twitched with anger; his top lip curled up over his smirk. "Yes, sir," he said.

10

After lunch Ed Ginsberg came out of the bookshop, his coat half on, old briefcase in his hand, looking up and down Twelfth Street for a cab. A dark blue car pulled up.

"Ed, Ed Ginthberg," came a high voice from the rear window.

"What? Who's that?" Ginsberg asked, crouching down to see in as the back door opened.

A hand reached out to shake his, grabbed and pulled. Someone else pushed him in from behind. He started shouting, but then a sack was on his head. The car pulled off; the door slammed. A hand like the back of an ax crashed on the base of his neck. Four hands pushed him to the floor of the car. A foot went in his groin, and his overcoat was twisted around his arms.

The foot in his groin stayed poised to crush him. He didn't dare move.

"Should we fuck him in the ath?" came the falsetto.

"No," answered an ordinary voice, "not yet. Let's hurt him first."

And then some sort of a stick or pipe crashed into his ribs. Tears came to his eyes. Then a fist into his stomach. Then he felt himself peeing in his pants.

When they started punching his mouth, when he started tasting the heavy, sweet blood, Ed kept thinking, I wonder if they're headed towards the auction, though he knew it didn't make sense.

Then everything went black, then red, then black.

~~~~~~ 11

"**C**ould you raise your arm a bit?" asked Harry, behind him, chalk in hand.

Sheridan raised it, felt Harry stop it and then make the chalk marks around the shoulder and under the arm of the sleeveless jacket. Was the business bothering him? Should it be? He'd never known any of them before, before looking down in that cold loft in Brooklyn and recognizing Horvay. Not exactly a shock. No particular acquaintance of his. Knew the gallery, had gone to one or two openings there, met at a few museum parties. Supposed to be some sort of Hungarian nobleman. "A count of no account," his mother would have said. The world wouldn't miss an art dealer.

"Yes, Harry," he smiled, slipping out of the jacket. He saw Harry put it on the tailor's dummy. It would be a very good suit.

No, Horvay was just another. They all fit the general proposition. People who had contracts taken out on them were no great loss. Scum, criminals. Hired, of course, by other scum. And he was the high-paid garbageman—no, what did they call themselves? Yes, "sanitary engineer." And the messenger? Well, he wasn't a contract, but that was self-defense. He'd decided that after the first-payment meeting with that twittering fairy. Sheridan adjusted the half-made-up trousers.

"Just the very slight break at the shoe top, sir?"

"Yes, fine," he said to Harry, now on his knees in front of him.

Sheridan wondered if whoever hired him was clever enough to count on his getting rid of the messenger, gratis, as it were? A risk of the trade. Perhaps it had been somewhat incautious to play with the body like that. Tricks like that were "signatures." There'd be no more of that. Still, it was a signature, too, to whoever'd hired him that he wasn't happy about the little green fairy, whatever their purposes in using him.

This was a good place to think it out. Sheridan smiled at the care Harry was taking with the chalk and pins. Harry had been his father's tailor, too.

"That will be all, Mr. Sheridan."

"Thanks, Harry. Two weeks?"

"Oh, yes, sir. Ten days or two weeks at the latest for the final fitting."

Dressing, Sheridan thought that knowing Horvay was a bit of bad luck. And it was also possible he might know who bought the contract. No knowledge was safest. But if one of the parties had to know, better *he* found out before the buyer did. It shouldn't be difficult to begin. His friends in the art world, a few natural enough questions at dinner. Yes, there was always someone like Bobo. Bobo Vandevelde might be useful.

12

Schwartz didn't like guns. He envied English police, who didn't carry them. If he had his way, the cops wouldn't carry them, the robbers wouldn't carry them, they'd be illegal to own in every corner of America, their manufacture would be illegal and the military would be much smaller so there'd be fewer guns there. But he didn't have his way. So he carried a gun and practiced on the police range when he was required to and was embarrassed because he was a fine shot. On duty he'd fired his police pistol twice in his seventeen-year career. He'd hit nothing, not counting himself when the second shot dislodged a bit of brick which flew off into his cheek, giving him a wound slightly smaller than a shaving nick.

Gallagher, who was no gun nut, figured the things were here to stay, so all you could do was try to keep them in the good guys' hands. "Oh, yeah, and gals." He'd wink if a policewoman were around. Gallagher practiced, enjoyed the occasion and was embarrassed because he was a lousy shot. He'd fired five times on duty in his career. Three of the shots killed an unsuccessful middle-aged hoodlum and saved Schwartz's life. But before he died, the hoodlum put two bullets into Gallagher, one in each lung. There was some infection, and it was a close thing.

Schwartz and Gallagher. The incident to Schwartz was a transcendent mystery of altruism. Thinking of it could still bring tears to his eyes. For Gallagher the whole subject was a pain in the ass, and he made Schwartz promise never to discuss it again.

Gallagher belonged to a private gun club. In their last years as partners he tried several times to convince Schwartz to join. Schwartz found the club amusing, "sociologically," as he put it, but he'd have none of it. He kept explaining his reasons to Gallagher, who kept asking, "Yeah, but *really* why won't you?" Since the bribe inquiry on Schwartz, the end of the partnership, Gallagher hadn't asked. When he thought of it, Gallagher was secretly glad Schwartz hadn't joined and even more secretly ashamed of being glad.

The club, in Greenwich Village, was officially named the Manhattan Pistol and Rifle Association, but it was known, affectionately or satirically or both, as the Small Bore Club. That was one thing Schwartz liked about it. Another was the building, a nice enough string of three old red-brick town houses, which had been, as he put it, wonderfully caca'd up by dense encrustations of brand-new old-fashioned lamps, metal marquees, concrete stone fountains running turquoise-tinted water, fake stone siding and white plastic window shutters. But most of all, Schwartz liked the membership, the idea of it. Where else in New York or the universe would a club mix high court judges with teamster union officials, merchant bankers with plumbing merchants, violent racists with token blacks and Hispanics, Zionist politicians with Syrian importers?

And, as Schwartz tried to explain, these were also the reasons why he wouldn't join. And the guns. All that noise in the basement.

So Gallagher had been surprised when Schwartz suggested they meet there.

"Yeah, sure. What's with you, Lenny?"

"The Horvay case. Something I don't want to talk about in your office or my office."

Gallagher sat at a corner table in the club's long dining room. It was filling for lunch. Someone from the DA's office waved to him. He got up and said hello to Tony DaPonte and Peter Frascatti and some other developers sitting with them. He sat down and nursed his drink. The commissioner of police came in with two borough presidents and was seated across the room. He'd go over and have a word later.

Schwartz came in scowling, saw Gallagher and walked past Louis, the headwaiter, who scowled, then smiled, turning to the next lunchers.

Gallagher stood and put out his hand. "Hi, Lenny. What the hell's up? You look terrible."

"You want to see someone who looks terrible, go over to Mount Sinai and see my old friend Ed Ginsberg. Teeth knocked out, slits for eyes in a face that looks like a big blue golf ball. Three cracked ribs, but that's the mild stuff. They're still checking for internal bleeding, wounds to organs—"

"OK, OK, I get the point. Tell me, but for Christ's sake, keep your voice down. People are eating."

Schwartz looked as if Gallagher had just suggested they send a two-ounce jar of caviar to Mother Teresa.

"Hey, Lenny, this is where you wanted to meet, remember? Lemme get you a drink. Still that campari and soda stuff?"

Schwartz ordered a large bourbon straight up and some unwanted lunch. Then he told Gallagher about his visit the morning before to the bookshop and later to the Stick Em Up.

"So you're saying it looks like they got to your friend after you went to the meat rack club? Have you pulled in that Anderson fag?"

"Sure, and a few of his boys. But we're not going to get anything from them. And if Ed pulls through . . . Jesus." Schwartz stopped and pushed the food around on his plate. "He won't be able to tell us anything. It's all too pat—it's so obvious, but there's nothing to tell. Look, Anderson had nothing to connect me with Ed Ginsberg. I went to see Ed before I went there. Anyhow, I would've gotten to the club without Ed's advice. No, it had to be a setup. This is about me, not about poor fucking Ed. They had to be following me."

"And why?" Gallagher asked, chewing thoughtfully.

"The obvious answer is to put me off."

" 'Cause you're coming close?"

Schwartz shook his head slowly, following his own thought. "And another obvious answer is to draw me on."

43

"They wouldn't want to."

"Exactly, Tom. They wouldn't. But whoever set up what could turn out the murder of one of my best friends—whoever that was would want it."

"Yeah? Still, the thing don't make sense."

Schwartz leaned across the table. His tie was in his creamed spinach, but Gallagher kept quiet.

"Tom, it doesn't make sense because this idea of yours that it's some sort of gay blackmail setup doesn't make sense."

"Could be. Hey, get your tie out of the spinach. Could be wrong, but you and I did pretty good as cops who kept plugging away at the obvious."

"And we were right. But remember how weird the obvious seemed? How we had to go out on a limb to defend it?"

Gallagher wiped his mouth and put down his napkin, smiling.

"Like," continued Schwartz, "the obvious but weird question I want answered is . . . is it you, Tom? You tailing me, setting me up for some—"

Gallagher's hand was around Schwartz's tie like iron, pulling him behind it. The fist let off, softened. "Here, you missed here," he said, red-faced, almost hissing, wetting a corner of his napkin in water and dabbing at the tie. "Listen, you wise son of a bitch, you made me lose my cool, and I don't like that. You wanna accuse me of shit like that, that what you really think? Do it. Get off your intellectual ass and cross this room and tell the commissioner over there. Make it a formal charge. But don't expect me to stoop to answer that. I'm sorry about your friend, Lenny, but shit, I'm on your side. I'm one of the good guys, remember?"

Schwartz fixed his necktie and looked down at the table.

"You wanna know about limbs? Jesus, you make me sick, having to say this stuff. You know the limb I went out on with him over there, the commissioner himself, to get you back into real detective work again? And I'm still out on it, and it's one goddamned long limb. Now."

Gallagher took a big breath. Schwartz took a big breath.

"All right, Lenny, so my theory's wrong. So what do you have?"

"Nothing. Some bits."

"And?"

"Just bits. If they fit anything, they fit your idea that Horvay bought it from the wild side." Schwartz pushed his chair back and put his hand out. "Tom. Sorry I said what . . . Ed's a close friend. . . ."

"I know. It's OK, Lenny. Whatever you need on finding who did him—you got it, you know that."

Gallagher watched Schwartz leave. The same tension in the walk he remembered back from when . . . By God, he wouldn't let that idealistic asshole upset his applecart. . . . Gallagher crossed the room and sat down to coffee with the commissioner of police.

$$\sim\sim\sim\sim \textbf{13}$$

He didn't want to tell Karen about Ed over the phone. Driving home, he rehearsed how he'd say it. He knew rehearsing was a bad sign. Nothing to do but blurt it out, the way he did anything that meant a lot. Why did it make him think of how shitty his relations with his son, Jake, had become? He could just call him at Yale, say hi. But no, let Jake call. Park Slope was hazy, pools of streetlight. He figured it was a certain sea fog only Brooklyn got. The streets looked nice. Quiet. Cozy neighborhood. No use: Ed's bruised purple head kept coming back.

Karen was at her desk, writing. She looked up. How beautiful she was. How she grew more beautiful. Schwartz bent over, his arms around her shoulders, his lips on her cheek.

Like other times, they didn't talk. Just stayed touching in the smell of the other's skin and hair, that warmth.

"Something terrible's happened. Ed Ginsberg's been beaten up."

Karen started forward under his arms, pulling away.

"As of an hour ago the hospital's sure he'll live. But he's in bad shape."

"Where? I mean, why, what happened?"

"Taken in the street, probably pushed into a car. Worked over by pros. Probably more than one. Forget the details. The worst is . . . Karen, Christ, I'm sure it was linked up to me questioning Ed about rough-trade gay clubs."

"Ed? Ed doesn't know anything. You know more than Ed. I know more!"

"I know I didn't have to. I feel so damned guilty." Schwartz's eyes began to swim.

Karen stood up. "Not your fault. Sit down. I'll get you a drink. Both of us."

Schwartz fell into the sofa and told her about Ed, the Stick Em Up giant, his festive lunch with Gallagher. And none of it really made sense.

Karen listened through the drink and through another drink. Then she said, "Inspector, stop thinking. Just sum it up. Put it into categories and forget about connections."

"Right. Horvay. Shot dead in an empty factory two weeks ago. Details not final but left over two million—after taxes. Very clear will: half a million to a sister in California—next of kin. No other family. The sister needs it like I need corns. Very rich. The rest goes into a trust for Cooper Union, where he'd been a fund raiser benefactor for years. Two assistants in the gallery. Clean. Seem genuinely sorry. Liked their jobs. The gallery's winding up into the estate. Papers, records being checked by whiz kid Bob. *Nada.* Horvay's private life—two parts. One involved with art world people—lots of high rollers, international museum crowd. Well liked there. The other, a fairly wild gay life . . . rough trade . . . details coming in now—tomorrow.

"OK," he continued, "then there's Parker, the jogger. Fifty-two, no criminal record. Lots of genteel jobs—salesman in Macy's, Bloomie's, various bookstores. Gay, disowned by the rest of his family, Baltimore Catholics. Lived alone, had occasional boyfriends—fellow salesmen, like that. Jobs a bit seedier in past four years—even some waiting in an East Side restaurant. Health-conscious, liked nice clothes. A fair amount of expensive new ones—the only possible . . . Oh, I'm not supposed to make connections. OK, and liked art—of the period Horvay dealt. No other link with him found. Yes, and a member of the Met with a whole collection of invitations to openings over the past two years. Checked out clean. Could have seen Horvay there with a thousand others. And then Ed, damn it. And that's it."

Karen sat thinking, looking somewhere beyond him. "Len," she said, "a few weeks ago I asked if you wanted me to snoop, find out about Horvay from my art world connections. You didn't answer then, so I didn't push. And I'm not pushing now, but I'm asking again."

He pursed his lips. "Yes. You're the professional in

that area, and I could use some loyal professional help. But carefully, no risks. You come across anything strange, you tell me at once. Back right off and tell me. This is the cop speaking."

"OK, cop. Let's have dinner now."

Schwartz went to sleep. Karen couldn't. She sat at her desk in front of the notes she was writing up. Maybe Len had wanted to make love. He hadn't said . . . Well, she couldn't, and that was that. The thought of Ed lying in Mount Sinai, barely alive. Ed was such a friend, so connected with her growing up; they'd always been able to talk across the stupid gender business because the sex wasn't there. Len was OK, good on that really, but it had been Ed who'd helped there, with sex, too, that . . . twelve years ago, that. It made them closer. Ed and Ben, Len and her. Oh, Ed. She felt the catch of tears under her heart, in her throat. And when she'd called, Ben said she couldn't even visit for a week.

She got up, put out the lights and went into the bathroom. Red eyes in the mirror. But why would they want to beat up Ed? Len was right. It was him they were getting at. Damn him. No, not his fault. Was he right, was it a setup?

The cold water felt good on her face, over her eyes. She'd see what she could do. Research was research, art history a sort of detective work. She'd see. It was the least she could do for Ed. Len. Ed.

BOOK II

———— 1

Georgia Morris had red hair. Sometimes people making small talk asked if she was called Scarlett, like Scarlett O'Hara. She said no, not bothering to point out their confusing "Georgia" with Scarlett and Scarlett with red hair. Scarlett had black hair. Georgia didn't like the movie or the book. She didn't like the sort of people who asked.

At twenty-nine Georgia Morris was curator and administrator of the Department of European Painting at the Metropolitan Museum of Art. It was a very good position in her profession, and she deserved it. She'd worked harder and been brighter than her male peers all along: in graduate school at Yale, at the Courtauld in London and now at the Met.

Not better than Bobo Vandevelde, but then he was her boss, not her peer. She liked working for him; he had a lot to teach her and was terrifically well connected with the sort of old-family people who sat on the boards that gave out the funds, and all that. Perhaps a bit too much the aesthete, not quite enough the administrator, but that was all right, too. She didn't see herself Vandevelde's assistant forever. She'd go higher than that. She wanted to be director of the Metropolitan. She'd have to wait, be better than any man at what she did. But she knew she could be. It wasn't vanity to have clear goals, not when you were capable of achieving them.

She'd been brought up not to be vain—not about her family, or her intelligence or her beauty. She had the redhead's fine bone-china skin—not white translucence but a delicate tan cream which grew dark in summer sunlight to a smooth nut brown. She was tall and slim without being skinny, and she worked on her body with the same bright energy she brought to anything worth her doing. It wasn't that all men turned as she walked by; her looks were too understated for that. But those who did, who looked close, were struck and charmed.

But she had no luck or, as she admitted to herself, little skill in relating to men. She'd had two lovers. The first, when she was nineteen at Bryn Mawr, was something of a playboy at Penn, one of those large, soft blonds she'd met at debutante balls. He'd been tender, doting and dull. The second had been a disaster, a middle-aged journalist in London. Very handsome, very fierce, a Greek Cypriote who gave her such sexual pleasure she followed him like a dog, and then he treated her like one. He ignored her, beat her and hurt her worse with his vicious tongue. And naturally he had a wife he wouldn't leave and three children he adored. Disaster.

She'd learned a lesson. She'd stick to her own kind, her own class and only single men. And if she couldn't find one, she'd just do without.

For instance, she caught herself smiling as she poured her orange juice, that man at the health club. What was it he reminded her of? She kept smiling—yes, of herself. Good looks that didn't push, the sensitive aloofness. Well, girl, she asked herself, are you going to do anything about it besides teasing at breakfast? Well, yes. Carefully.

2

Sheridan wasn't sure. Bobo Vandevelde didn't give anything away. Just strange, that word *Why?* from such an articulate man.

Sheridan had made it seem he'd run into Dickie Fairchild at the club, said he'd like to see him again, and true to form, Dickie invited him to one of his fund-raising parties, one of those Save Venice dos. A tax deduction for guests which he was sure ended in some Italian senator's bank account. Still, there were Bobo and Honey Vandevelde—he elegant, she still handsome in faded Fortuny silk.

He'd been put with Honey at a dinner table for six and didn't even have to bring up Horvay himself; someone else did. Then he'd asked Honey if they'd known him well. And off she trotted into her gossipy chat, amusing enough in a dusty way, not that she had anything to tell him. Thought his death was connected to his "wanting to live in Gotham and Sodom at the same time," as the press suggested with less assonance.

And afterwards, chatting with Bobo, Sheridan had said, "Honey's in great form. I was asking her about Alex Horvay."

"Why? I mean, what were you asking?"

Not even a change in tone, but the *why* and then the change to *what* stayed in Sheridan's mind.

"Just the usual, Bobo. You know. Poor old Alex. Who could have killed him, had him killed, such a tragedy. It's crazy."

"I liked him, Johnnie. Of course, I knew he had that homosexual, night side to his character. But as for the Hungarian business, I was going to say 'gay Hussar' but thought it in questionable taste, considering. No, he was just a bit dramatic and used it when he started up here, after he left, fled, Hungary in '56. Did you know that?"

"No, I'd only met him once or twice at openings."

"Well, he was unfairly made fun of. Whatever his private life, I think everyone in the business found him honorable and fair—though he drove some hard bargains."

"So I suppose that's it: he ran afoul of some killer queen."

Vandevelde shook his head in distaste. "Yes. Look at that fine little Van Ruisdael beside the mantelpiece. Wonderful. Dickie bought that from poor old Alex."

A waiter stopped by with a tray of cognac and champagne. Neither took any. The painting made Sheridan remember the smell of a Dutch canal on a gray-blue November day. Then of other canals, heat and palm trees and water to his chin. He nodded to Bobo and moved off into the party, thinking that yes, on the whole it would be best to keep tabs on him. It wouldn't be hard; it would be rather pleasant.

3

At the end of the party Vandevelde was speaking with Dickie Fairchild in the library of his fourteen-room Park Avenue duplex.

"And terrific seeing Johnnie again. He's become such a recluse. How'd you get him to come?"

"Ran into him at the Union Club the other day. He was terribly friendly, for him, I mean. Anyhow, he suggested we get together, so of course, I asked him over. Still clips the coupons, does he?"

"I suppose so. But he's a clever investor, I've heard. Does very well in that mysterious way of his."

"Yes. Still in shape, too. Must be one of the more eligible bachelors in town."

Later, after saying good night to Honey, Vandevelde lay in his bedroom wondering if Johnnie Sheridan was up to something and, if so, what?

~~~~~~~ **4**

Changing at her locker, Georgia began having doubts. How could she do it? She could look and smile, but if he didn't say anything it wouldn't work. She could pretend to be confused by the equipment and ask him how it worked, but that depended on an attendant's not being there when and if he walked through. No, too slight a chance. Haven't we met before? Oh, Lord, how corny! She couldn't.

Ten minutes later, working out at the machine, she'd decided to forget it. And there he was, coming into the room. She pushed faster and looked straight ahead.

"Excuse me."

She stopped and turned her head.

"You're Georgia Morris, aren't you? I'm John Sheridan, a friend of Gerald Vandevelde. We met, last year, I believe."

"So that's it. Hello. I thought you looked familiar," Georgia laughed. "I'd been thinking how to say hello to you, but I couldn't work it out."

"A plain 'hello' would've done fine. Do you have time for coffee at the bar here after you work out?"

"Yes. In twenty-five minutes?"

"Good," said John.

"Good," said Georgia.

They had coffee, later that week they had dinner, and on Friday night they went to a play, looked at each other at the end of the first act, walked out and took a cab to John's apartment. They said very little, their hands coming together lightly but with such hot energy that Georgia felt her heart throbbing, pushing her dress against her coat.

And in the elevator of the large mews house, his hand under her coat arm made her mouth tremble. By the time they were in the apartment and John had taken her coat off, Georgia felt nearly sick with, it seemed to her, excitement.

"Johnnie, listen, I'm so—I've told you how long it's been since I've made love. Something—I just need to sit still for a minute. I don't want to pass out before—" Georgia broke off, embarrassed. She didn't look around her, took nothing in.

He brought brandy. She drank it and felt better. He sat and looked at her with an amused tolerance she didn't want to see as condescension. But he had great physical tact. She liked that, and when she smiled, he came over and sat beside her on the sofa and kissed her, not as he had that first time, strangely shy and formal like a young boy, but kissed with his tongue moving lightly around the rim of her full lips and then into her mouth so that their tongues ran top to top, back and across each other, tingling, driving down into her breasts, nipples, into his hands so lightly on her back.

"Let's . . ." was all he said, and they were up and seemed suddenly in the bedroom undressing themselves, each other. It was like a trance, but a trance in which all her senses were heightened. She saw the texture of skin on a body larger, more muscled than she'd imagined. She looked at the light hair on his chest and between his legs and seemed to taste it before she touched it.

His hands stopped on her thigh, his fingers circled the golden freckle marks on the white inside flesh. His hands went behind her. He lifted her; she felt weightless. He set her down. His mouth played over the small of her throat, moved to her breasts; his tongue licked around the base of her nipples. Her hand touched the fine cloud of brown hair on his balls. His fingers reached down to her pubis, moved the red-haired mound up over the bone, spreading the folds, pulling back the folds so lightly, with such electric tenderness on and around and just there on her clitoris. And then it was his tongue, and it covered her vulva, slid down, up to there, there, again such huge tiny shocks of pleasure. Her hands reached down through his hair, pulled down his neck, pulled up on the heavy sinew of his shoulders, sliding him up and over her until his mouth was on hers, and she licked it and the bottom of his nose, and now he entered her and he was moist, smooth and he felt like velvet in the silk of her vagina.

Filled, filled in and entering and full. Big but wonderfully, not stick-hard—thick, limber. She arched and slid, and his hands dug in, one on her shoulder, one into the flesh of her hips and moved her, moved her faster and now breathless, the thrill wave building each time. Building. She screamed coming, ran her nails up his big back coming, felt him coming that hot filling, kept screaming coming. Still but falling away but still waves less but coming, down down.

"Oh, my God," she said. "Oh, Johnnie, my darling. Oh, my God."

He relaxed on her. She hugged him to her, felt the size and power of him, felt covered entirely as if she were in him. The sweat on her fingers in the furrow of his spine. His light down.

Later she woke, stretched, looked at him sleeping, looking twenty, not forty. He had long eyelashes, she saw now. He was beautiful. She was thirsty, looked around, got up and went naked into the bathroom. Drinking the cold late-winter water, she realized she had no idea of where she was, that nothing had registered but him, her, that physical joy. Georgia smiled, laughed out loud. Ran her hand through her thickly tangled still-damp hair.

She went back into the bedroom, saw his silk bathrobe on the chair and wrapped it round her.

She looked at him asleep. The mysterious Johnnie Sheridan! She knew fifty women in New York who'd kill to . . . what did it matter? Still, she felt a pride. What didn't he have: family, money, brains, taste, oh yes, such a taste, such a body, a lover. Her hands inside the bathrobe pockets crossed each other, wrapped round her.

She walked out of the bedroom. And so this was where he lived. Wonderful, like him. It must be the entire upper floor, floors? of the old red brick mews house, the kind she always thought were fire stations. Wide hallways, in which she made out walls of bookcases. A living room the size of a small church, the furniture old, leather, a bit clubby. Her father would have loved this room, the far end raised a few steps, the books and books and . . . She went over to the wall. It was. Goodness, it was a Claude Lorrain. And the others . . . oh, she'd have to really look at these. The photos . . . there he was, at Harvard, on a boathouse dock. Why couldn't I have met him then? Now what do I mean? I would have been nine or ten! Nice Chinese bronze, too.

She walked slowly, trailing her fingers over the surfaces of the rooms, his rooms, the touch of his . . . Like that scene in *Queen Christina* where Garbo, after the night at the inn, goes around touching, touching. Her hand pushed open a door. She followed it through, felt for the light switch.

His study, office, a business library. A modern man in here, she thought. The computer, screen, stacks of software. A library table, photos. This? She picked up the silver frame. Who was that in uniform, black grease over his face, a woods? in a beret. Him? A rifle pointing down to something, the photo clipped by the frame, she—

"Oh!" She jumped at the touch on the back of her neck.

"Shh. It's only me."

His voice. His hand stayed on the back of her neck, turned her towards him. Pulled her head into his chest. She kissed it. The hair in her mouth, the nipple hard on his hard breast. She felt strange, heavy-headed, sleepy. Something he was doing with his fingers on the back of her neck. Some memory, idea about the photo passing, passed. His strong steel fingers rubbed gently, and Georgia passed into sleep.

―――――――― **5**

Georgia had met Karen Walker; she'd met most of the people in the fine arts world once or twice. Until last year she'd placed Karen in the second rank of art historians: a deep, steady, scholarly cast of mind in good but infrequent monographs on Impressionists and Postimpressionists. But that was before the publication of *Reflections of Monet's Garden*, a fine, no, a really brilliant work, showing the influence of Colombe-les-Église on the most unexpected painters, especially Gauguin and Cézanne. The scholarship was massive, painstaking, and the book was better than well written. A major talent had emerged. So when Karen Walker called and invited her to lunch, Georgia was interested; when she said she wanted to pick her brain, Georgia was fascinated.

They met at the bar in Dinah's, one of the new restaurants in old showrooms around Union Square. The formula was large columns, long bar, heavy pink linen tablecloths and vase after vase of strikingly unfamiliar flowers.

First, each found the other more beautiful than either remembered—the tall, fine-boned redhead, the voluptuous brunette. Next, each found the other articulate and funny. Then, over lunch, each found the other wary.

Finally, about the time both were smiling at the sameness of the restaurant's originality, Georgia said, "Well?"

"Well? Well. Yes, why we're here—besides the flowers and waiter's recital of the specials. Well, would the Met have done business with . . . I mean, do you know anything about that murdered art dealer Alex Horvay?"

"That's not your line, is it?" Georgia asked, lifting the glass of white wine to her mouth.

"No. I'm doing some research. Not exactly. Look, it's something that just fascinates me, why someone would kill a man like Horvay, have him killed. It's just a personal—"

"That's all right. I knew him, of course, and I knew, like many did, that he was gay and liked rough trade. That is, I heard it from a friend who knew. Alex never told me. But I gather he was quite open about it to closer acquaintances. So my guess would be that the papers have it right, more or less . . ."

Karen asked, "But the museum?"

67

"Oh, we bought one or two small works from Horvay over the past ten or fifteen years. His big sales were to smaller museums and big private collectors."

"Was there ever anything special—strange—about his dealings: import or insurance problems, passing fakes? I know these sound like strange questions, but . . . Oh, listen, I can't go on like this. My husband's on the case."

"The case? . . . Your husband is a policeman?"

Karen frowned and smiled at the same time. "An inspector of detectives. Yes, a policeman."

Georgia looked down. "Sorry for the snobbery. It's just surprising. Are you working on this—"

"Oh, no. I'm just doing some looking around on my own, unofficially. But of course, I'll tell Len, my husband, if I find anything."

"But doesn't he do his own work and you yours?" Georgia asked, the amused distance returning to her voice.

"Of course. But wouldn't you do what you could in the circumstance?"

Georgia thought about it for a moment. "I have no way of knowing. But I think not. Well, as far as I recall, Horvay was totally aboveboard. I could find out more; there's a research office I could use, check it, that sort of thing."

"That would be good of you"—Karen paused—"though I don't know why you should."

"Because I admire your book. And you. And because we're women."

Karen smiled. "Thanks. And look, keep it low-key. You understand."

"Of course. Detectives and all that." And Georgia smiled back, thinking, What a bit of fun. She'd have to tell Johnnie about it.

~~~~~~~~ **6**

Schwartz was depressed by the mass of evidence piling up. It was third-rate. Big Cal Anderson had become wonderfully cooperative, and they'd come up with fifteen people who had motives to kill Horvay, or Hooray, as these suspects knew him. The motives were sex, madness, drug-induced madness, sex-induced madness and sex- and drug-induced madness. And one case of what Schwartz thought clinical paranoid schizophrenia, a term the department was happy to use, he noted, now that it was professionally suspect and passé. Still, they were changing faster than the Vatican. Another idea he didn't bother sharing at work.

The motives stank—stank as motives, too. Some rough customers, but junkies, petty crime boys, thugs capable of beating Horvay to death with a chain or gang-banging him to death. But not that neat, professional killing. And none of them had the money for that sort of hit man. And only one of them knew of Horvay's real name and daytime existence. And this one blurted, weeping, that he'd come across the gallery and looked in to see "crazy Alice." And crazy Alice had given him *such* a look. Well, one understands. I mean, he sniffed, life's hard enough for us without blowing any whistles on each other. Yes. They were all small-timers.

"Hey, Bob."

"Yessirlen." Bob's head around the door, his big, bony body following. A puppy dog.

"No. Not Sir Len. I haven't been knighted, Mr. Malinowski." Schwartz watched Bob smile and nod, as if taking in an important fact.

"Bob, you ever hear of hit men working like lawyers, on spec? You know, taking nothing or little for killing but working on a percent of the final take?"

Bob was quiet, eyes down to the floor. He might have been pondering an elliptical statement in Wittgenstein. Jesus, thought Schwartz, if he doesn't *look* something like Wittgenstein.

"No, sir." Bob looked up. "Not a real contract killer. It's always strictly payment before or after, or both. Otherwise, it's someone involved in the whole thing that does the killing." He finished, trying to suppress a pride like that of a cat laying a dead bird at your feet.

Why, Schwartz wondered, did he think all these things about Bob, whose only sin was being in awe of him? "Sit down, Bob, sit down."

Schwartz ducked out and brought back two coffees.

"No, sit, Bob. Here. If I haven't already told you, you're doing a damn good job for me. You're really pulling together all the forensics, the statements and the other bits just as well as they could be, uh, pulled together."

"Thanks, sir." Bob sat with his big hands covering the cup, steam coming through his fingers, blushing. "That means a lot to me."

"Listen, Bob, you're no hotshot, and you're a better cop for it. I'm the hotshot. And I can't make anything of this case."

"We just have to keep working with the facts. I mean, I do. I wish . . ."

"Don't. I'm no model cop. Anyhow, you do that, you keep sifting. I have to go another way, and don't ask me what, because I don't know. So if Gallagher or any of his gang asks, you can tell them that's all you know," Schwartz said, going to the coatrack, "and you'll be telling the whole truth."

"Why are they keeping so close on this, sir? It's not that we're lazy."

"True. I hate to be my own iconoclast, Bob, but I think they don't trust me."

"Sir?"

"No," Schwartz said, putting on his coat, "it's Lenny," and walked out.

He stood outside in the cold winds off both rivers and thought he'd been too hard on Bob Malinowski. Then he thought how lucky he was to have Bob around. Then he thought that the right thing to do would be to have Bob drive around with him so he could see the "great" intuitive process at work. He looked at the car, thought, The hell with it, and walked off towards the subway.

It wasn't even a hunch, nothing but a funny lethargy that had kept him, all these weeks, from doing the fairly obvious talking with other gallery owners about Horvay. And yet, for all the pushing, prodding and generally spying helpfulness of Gallagher's office, neither Tom nor his minions had suggested it. Never mentioned it. Interesting? Not quite yet it wasn't.

Half an idea. He changed at Union Square for the Lexington Avenue uptown express.

The train seemed half full of beggars and half full of businessmen. A one-legged black man, silent but for the shaking of his paper cup, eloquent with the small sign I LOST IT IN VIETNAM, BOSS. The businessmen behind the *New York Times*. Schwartz dropped some change in.

Another one, one of his favorites, the blind white singer with the big dog, the spiel about changing the law for the blind with dogs on the subways, the little amplifier and smaller tenor voice sweetly warbling Italian bel canto. He did better than the legless black. Hands came out from behind *Wall Street Journals*, relieved, noted Schwartz, to be able to feel pity without guilt. Plink, plunk, in the metal cup. His plunk, too. Poor women, he'd noticed, poor Hispanic and black women gave most. Well, you could take the sociologist from Chicago but not the University of Chicago dropout sociologist from the failing cop.

What was it? Something he hadn't felt for years . . .

He got out at Grand Central, didn't have to. Went to the middle of the platform. Waited, not really looking, for the local. Waited till the doors were closing, put his hand in, held there, got in. Stood in the crowded car not looking at anything in particular. Yes, there, a glimpse two cars away. Got out at Fifty-ninth, slowly up the stairs then, at the turn, fast up, pushed past, turned right, through the doors out of the subway urine smell into Bloomingdale's perfumes.

Schwartz didn't look back, had moved just too slowly, obviously, to lose the pro tailing him. Walked through the glass and bottle glitter purposefully. Then, what? He knew. He went down to the mezzanine level by a staircase, walked through it past the sign to the snack bar, past the sign apologizing for the inconvenience in redecorating. Plywood panels, hanging bundled wires. Schwartz turned at the snack bar into more temporary corridors, passed the bookstore entrance, no one here now. Yes, this would do, an opening, overlap between two plywood sheets. Behind were tools, electrical supplies, bags of concrete on a concrete floor. He put his ear to the plywood. Nothing. Yes, now, long steps and quiet enough. Good shadow, but not good enough.

The footstep passed. Schwartz jumped out, tripped the tall man, got him in a half nelson on the floor. A small woman started screaming. The tall man was pulling at a blue wool cap. Strong mother. Brought his free hand back, pulled Schwartz's ear. Schwartz rolled off. His hand chopped out at the tall man's neck as he got up, sinking him back down to his knees.

"Stop! Stop dis!" the woman was screaming. "Enimals! Stop!" she screamed.

He was getting up. Schwartz pulled at his ankles. He fell back down onto Schwartz.

"No, sir, sir."

Schwartz heard screaming, got the stranglehold.

Gasping sounds, they rolled on the floor. "Shrr, srr."

"Grown men, like enimals. Vere . . ."

"Malinowski! What the fuck!"

They were sitting on the floor at the little woman's feet. Bob held his neck, rasping.

"Disgusting enimals!"

"Shut up, lady. Please. Police." Schwartz put his hand in for his wallet. "Here, I'll show you."

"Don't show me notink, enimals!"

He flashed the badge.

"So, police?"

"Yes," Schwartz said, "move away. We're both police."

"Both? Vonderful! Vonderful! Ve ain't got enough crime, you gotta be fightink each other now?"

"Away, please. Madam."

She backed away. "Enimals!"

He looked at Bob. "And you, what the fuck do you think you're doing?"

"Listen, such lengvidge!"

"I was worried," gasped Bob. "I thought I'd better follow you."

"Worried! Worried, my ass. You followed me because Tom Gallagher ordered you to follow me!"

"No, sir. I swear!" Bob said in great air-sucking sobs.

Schwartz looked at him. Tears were rolling down the big face. Tears, for Christ's sake. Shit.

"Even when I'm choking you to death, you call me

sir. Can't you call me Lenny *then,* you goddamned idiot!"

"Yes, sir."

The two policemen on the floor, one red from strangulation, the other from rage.

"Enimals." The old woman sighed, walking away.

7

"That's a funny story. What's the matter with you, Len? How can you tell me about a life-and-death struggle with Bob Malinowski at Bloomingdale's and not find it funny?" Karen looked at Schwartz.

Schwartz looked at the knuckles he kept cracking.

Karen said, "It's not the sound. It's the sound connected to what you're doing. And it's not what you're doing. It's what you're doing connected to the state you're in. That's what gets to me."

Schwartz said, "Oh. Yes," and continued cracking his knuckles.

Karen jumped up, put her arms behind her and paced in front of the armchair like a burlesque district attorney. "All right, Schwartz. The credo! Let's have it," in a voice that sneered and drawled.

Schwartz looked up. "What?"

"C'mon, c'mon, Schwartzie. The credo. The credo. Don't play dumb with me. All right!" She spun and leaned over him. "Out with it. What's the worst thing that can happen to a cop? Well? Well?"

He nodded and said, in a straight-faced monotone, "The worst thing that can happen to a cop is that he thinks everyone except a cop is wrong."

Karen walked away, turned on her heel and pointed two fingers. "And the second? C'mon, don't hold out on me, Schwartzie, the second?"

"The second worst thing," he said, starting to smile, "that can happen to a cop is that he thinks everyone except a cop is right."

"Yeah?" Karen sneered. "And why is the second not so bad as the first?"

Schwartz nodded, smiling. "Because it never happens."

"Because it never happens! Your Honor," Karen said, turning to the record collection with a flourish, "I rest my case."

"It's sweet of you, but it doesn't work anymore. Besides, to tell you the truth, I feel that maybe everyone *is* right except me. But I won't crack my knuckles any—"

"Don't patronize me. It's not the knuckle cracking. I just told you. And I don't care about being sweet. The truth could also be that the credo's right and you're right."

"Oh? Ah. Cops never think they're wrong; I think I'm wrong. *Ergo*—I'm no cop. Yes, could be. Then, in my defense—"

"Wait," Karen interrupted, the pain showing in her

face, "I'm not the prosecution. I'm on your side." She turned her desk chair towards Schwartz and sat down.

"Karen, as I was saying. In my defense, there's this five-year retirement—I don't think that's a bad name for it—that I've just come off, so maybe I've lost my touch."

"Come on, Len. Let's have it out."

"Sure," he said, crossing his legs as if settling in for a comfortable debate.

"You haven't lost your touch. For what I'm worth as an interested outsider, you seem to be going about business now much as you used to. Preoccupied, touchy, apparently lost in the data but pushing with—no, it's more than intuition, it's the way your intelligence is creative. So you're pushing towards whatever it is that will break the case. You think you've lost some confidence, but all you've lost in the past five years is your old partner, Tom. Does that scare you?"

Schwartz looked at Karen, thinking, then answered, "No. But that was a good question, good to hear it out and ask it myself, out loud. No. Gallagher was a good partner, but there was all that tension, too. And whatever I may say, Bob's coming along. We're a good inside/outside team. And no more of Gallagher's racism and palism to screw me around."

"So?"

"Oh, come on, Karen, if we're having it out, we're having it out. Five years ago I was an honest cop. Today I'm a crook with a badge. As simple as that."

"It's sending Jake through Yale."

"Funny, five years later and we're arguing opposite sides."

"No. I'm just reminding you of what it was for—from your point of view."

"It. It." Schwartz uncrossed his legs, leaned forward. "The bribe, the seventy-five-thousand-dollar bribe from the cocaine dealer. I'm sick of hiding behind pronouns."

"You took it. You asked me—I said don't. But you took it, and I stayed with you. So I guess I took it, too. Lived with it, too."

"Interesting," said Schwartz, settling back into the cross-legged position again as if he meant "interesting." "In a way it's been terrific for your career. You started working on the book as a way of dealing with our problem—losing yourself in work. And now you're the art success of the season, the year. A celebrity."

Karen stood up. She gripped the seat back. "You . . . you damned infant. Of course, I lost myself, but if you think I didn't have it in me but for . . . I mean, what are you saying now—you took the bribe for my career?"

"I didn't say—"

"No, but just as dumb." Her hand opened and pulsed closed around the wood. "And if I have some small, small celebrity in a small professional world, why should you be jealous? What's happened to you—the old friend of the feminist? Who encouraged me more than Ed and you? Not anyone else, not even Molly."

"Keep your mother out—"

"Stop it, you ass. I'm saying something good." She let go of the chair and threw herself onto Schwartz's lap. "Len, what? What is it?"

"That funny way I work, you know. Well, it's working. I'm beginning to sense things with—what did you say? as if I forgot—that creative intelligence of mine," he said in his business monotone, his arms around Karen's waist.

"What things?"

"I'm not sure what kind of a crime I'm involved with exactly, but I have a good idea that one of the people involved in a criminal cover-up is in the department."

"Oh, baby!" Karen said, turning her amazement into comfort.

"Way up high. Maybe bigger. Bigger than hustling Tom Gallagher, though he's in on it. But for now, the worst of it is Bob Malinowski."

"But you said you believed him telling you he'd followed you from his own feeling that you were in danger."

"He did. That's the trick—how they've gotten to him. I'm his idol. So he's a natural to watch me, by protecting me."

"From what?"

"From themselves."

8

Schwartz made no appointments with the galleries. He walked in off the street, another looker. He walked around, looked at the art, the catalog, the price list, and only afterwards went up to the person at the desk and asked to speak to the owner. Sometimes he found he was speaking to the owner.

Sometimes, usually if it wasn't the owner, a cool eye would be raised and a cold voice ask, "Concerning what?" The eyes and voice warmed up when Schwartz opened the badge wallet and said, "Concerning this." Everyone was so cooperative.

Everyone in old masters knew Horvay. Or knew of him. Few knew him personally. And one after another gave the same opinion: Horvay was clean, quality, a model of making it. One or two knew he was gay; one, himself gay, even knew Horvay "partied rough," thought him a fool to do it and thought his murder was the risk he ran. When Schwartz suggested that it probably was not a contract taken out by any of Horvay's S & M partners, the owner became offended, told Schwartz there were plenty of gays who could afford such a thing, told Schwartz he should be careful of stereotyping, remembered whom he was talking to and apologized. Schwartz told him there was no need and he certainly would be careful of stereotyping, thanked him for his cooperation and left.

Four o'clock on Madison Avenue. A gray day in early March that could have been early anything from November on. Stereotyping—"Certain gays are not rich" is a stereotype? Sometimes his job was so silly he liked it. He went into a coffee shop and looked at the list Karen had made. One more today. Best for last, what could be called Horvay's competitor.

Two tables away sat the sort of person who helped make Schwartz's day. A New York Character. This one definitely the very top end of the scale; not just a well-dressed WASP, your actual dandy. But a dandy, thought Schwartz, not a fop. A fop was what, a flopped dandy? A foolish dandy with a low IQ? He'd better stay off the IQ business to keep from stereotyping. The IQ was now proved the work of racist charlatans. How proud he'd been of Jake's.

He hoped Jake didn't go into the art gallery business. Or become a cop. No fear of that. Jake, he figured, was ashamed of his dad's being a cop. Would *he* have been? Probably, yes. Not many cops' kids at Yale. Nor many union organizers' kids at Harvard in his day. More like—Schwartz looked at the dandy.

Jesus, he looks like someone at Harvard, one of those clubby types we all hated and were jealous of.

And Jake hadn't even called since going back to New Haven in January. How can Karen be so cool about it? She was right. What would Jake think if he knew about the money? Would young Jake Schwartz keep carrying on like young Jock Whitney if he knew he was carried on a coke bribe? Did Jake do coke? Stop it. Don't play the inspector with your son. But if I told him? Is it a cop-out to tell him? A cop-out not to? Some word for moral cowardice—cop-out!

Schwartz was walking up Madison.

On the street the David Sylvester Gallery was one small glass case in bronze by a large bronze door. In the crushed brown velvet lining the case a card framed in old walnut said "Recent Acquisitions." Schwartz had the feeling he couldn't have afforded the frame. Through the bronze door a small lobby ended in another bronze door, this one for an elevator. By its side a security man at a table. Serious security, Schwartz noted, flashing his badge at the guard, who wasn't fat or feeble, like so many. And TV monitors. One inside the elevator, too. No use playing the tourist. The doors slid open onto another pair. They slid open into the gallery.

A woman in a gray flannel suit stood up, smiled a gray flannel smile and asked him if he'd like a catalog, as if she hadn't seen him on the monitor or had the call from downstairs that a cop—no, here it would be a "police officer"—was coming up.

"Len Schwartz. Police Department," he said, again

showing the badge. "I'd like to talk to David Sylvester about Alex Horvay."

"David's in Europe, Mr. Schwartz. I'm Angela Sylvester. David's my husband. I'll be able to talk to you about Alex." She paused. "I'm a partner in the gallery, in case you're wondering if I'll do." She smiled the cold gray smile again.

"Fine with me."

"Let's go into the office," she said, leading Schwartz.

The gallery wasn't so special. The Frick was more elegant, the Met was bigger, he thought, trailing over the Aubussons that stretched over the marble.

Above, great tan shades were drawn up under the skylights. The paintings on the wall looked familiar or as if they should be familiar. The recent acquisitions, no doubt.

They went through an oak door into a different world, a no-nonsense business office. Four desks, three women and one man at work, two at computer displays. Bright-looking, well dressed. No one even looked up. Then another door and a room that was a fair mix between the outer office and the gallery—no-nonsense and some really fabulous nonsense. It was decorated in early understatement.

"Sit here, please," she said, taking the chair opposite. She smiled that smile that he didn't like. "This must be different from your usual, ah, sphere of work."

Schwartz looked at her dully, without saying anything. She fidgeted in the chair. She crossed her legs. Schwartz looked at her legs. Then he said, "That's right. I don't usually sit around on a Louis Treize chair with mostly original gros point, except here," and he pointed to a corner of the back. "The taxpayers might think it a bit extravagant."

Her smile had changed to something else.

"So now that we have all the chips off our shoulders, let's talk, Ms. Sylvester. We have a pretty full biography of Horvay, know he was liked in the business—well respected. Kept kosher." He watched Angela Sylvester's eyes narrow at his expression and enjoyed it. "So let's save each other's time and please don't tell me how nice or how foolish Horvay was. Was he honest?"

"Yes. Is that direct enough, Officer? Or is it Detective?"

"Yes. Direct enough. And let's be relaxed about this, Angela. Please call me . . . Mr. Schwartz. So how'd he do so well?"

She glared at him. "I think there were several reasons. He had an engaging personality, real charm—so he was a good salesman. Then he really knew his field. He was well traveled, well connected, and he had a good nose, a good intuitive sense, Mr. Schwartz. Then, too, he was lucky, Mr. Schwartz, very lucky, though of course, I speak as an envious competitor."

"What do you mean by 'lucky'?"

She leaned forward a bit and suddenly came to life. She happened, Schwartz found himself thinking, to be a very beautiful woman made unattractively brittle by an armor of ice. Perhaps a sexist observation, he thought, but true.

"You, and I do mean *you*, probably know that most of our trade is in known work: Collector A sells work X; the B collection containing work Y is to be auctioned. That sort of thing. Of course, we're always snooping here and there, establishing contacts, networks, in the hope that we'll come up with something new. That is, something old—but new to the market. Very, very occasionally we do. But it's a great coup. Obviously the profit is attractive enough to keep us going. Would you like a coffee, anything to drink?"

Schwartz asked for a coffee he didn't really want. The gray flannel lady had turned disturbingly to flesh. What the hell was it with him? He never played these games. He watched her move to a coffee maker. She was, he'd say, in her midthirties and had this smooth, white, alabaster skin. That was it, like a statue. A Victorian statue, the nose straight down from the forehead. Burne-Jones or Rossetti painted such.

"No milk or sugar, thanks."

She sat down and he looked away. Into his coffee cup. But he heard the nylons swish as she crossed her legs. Stop it, Schwartz. White, alabaster legs.

"Go on. How was Horvay different?"

"For the last ten years—no, even longer—since, I think, the early seventies he had one after another of the most marvelous finds: Troost, De Wit, Bakhuysen, Cuyp and both Van Ruisdaels. Extraordinary luck."

"Just luck? Was there ever any other, uh, interpretation?"

"You mean, were there forgeries? No. This trade depends upon absolute confidence and reliability. No. These were authenticated not just by Horvay, expert enough, but by others. No, just extraordinary luck."

"What others?"

"Other experts, the leading world authorities. Gerald Vandevelde, for instance. Probably the genre's leading authority."

"Vandevelde. Sounds like one of the painters," he said.

"At least two had that name. I think Bobo might be some distant relation of Willem, the marine painter."

"Bobo?"

"Bobo, Gerald Vandevelde. He's chairman of European Painting at the Met."

"Very impressive. Thanks. You've been helpful. I'm sorry about, well . . ."

She stood and put out her hand, which wasn't ice cold at all. "Me, too. Forgive me. It's just somehow got to me, I'm afraid, having two people ask the same questions in one day."

"Has another policeman been here?"

"No. It was this morning. Karen Walker, the art historian. You know, she's written that book—have I said something funny, Mr. Schwartz?"

~~~~~~ **9**

Georgia kept telling herself to "take it easy, girl, relax, go slow," but her heart raced to think of Johnnie. She'd never met, never imagined anyone could be so steady and quiet and exciting. He was—well, wild, she'd say to herself, lowering her head to smile over her desk. And driving her wild, but not the bad old London way. Without the macho histrionics of the Greek who made her feel how much she owed him for any pleasure he gave, Johnnie gave and gave and . . . She shook her head, smiling. What he did with his tongue and his lips. Oh, Lord, she knew she couldn't get down to work thinking like this.

And then the adventure. Not that she'd made love before only under the sheets. But how he'd touch her in public, his hand in her pants under the tablecloths of smart restaurants, or how he'd just appeared in that

changing booth at Bergdorf's and forever changed
Bergdorf's for her. How she found herself shivering
with what he told her to do and she couldn't imagine
anyone so strong, standing up holding her hips around
him back and forth like that. And she loved him
because if she was too frightened, he would let it go
and be his elegant, kind self. But the fright was mixed
up more and more with the thrill so that at Sloane's in
that corner piled with Chinese carpets they'd just looked
at each other and he nodded and she'd slid off her
pants and he was on the carpets first so she climbed
onto him. . . . She shut her eyes and saw the cream
carpet, and again its blue-flowered border came closer,
receded, came closer again, again.

She opened her eyes and looked up into the cluttered silence of her office. Yes, she loved him. Damn
it, she hadn't wanted anything like this so fast, but
there—she'd said it and it was true. But she wouldn't
say it to him. She vowed he'd have to say it first. She
vowed. Then she thought how she loved him besides
the sex. He was strong, and bright and well bred and
just strong in everything he did. He didn't seem to
care much for children, but that was all right. She had
her career, too, and there was only Mother now in
Philadelphia. But how nice to hear the interest in her
voice when she'd told her whom she was seeing.

"Grosvenor Sheridan's boy? Oh, Georgie. He's what
would have been called quite a catch in my day, darling. Fine family, Anglo-Irish, not shanty-Irish, all the
difference. Someone—was it your aunt Phyllis?—told
me something, years ago now about young John being
some sort of war hero. But surely too young for World

War Two?" And on she'd natter, so pleased to at last have something important to talk about with her modern, "too modern if you ask me," daughter.

Georgia stood up, walked about the office, put her hands into her jacket pockets and twirled around. Like a schoolgirl, she thought. And then: And what's wrong with that? And he was so—nice. Stupid word, trite word, but there was no other word for him.

Like that business with Karen Walker wanting to dig into Alex Horvay's murder. A clever woman like that married to a policeman. Beyond understanding. Well, it was fun snooping around, and Johnnie was so nice and helpful, offering to put anything she could find into his computer, though what the computer could make of it was more than she knew.

More than John Sheridan knew. What he knew was that there were only two ways in this business: knowing nothing or knowing everything. Knowing a bit was dangerous. And since he knew a bit, he'd better find out the rest.

Georgia was fine; better than he could reasonably have hoped. And that woman coming to her for help.

It was better, it was amusing, his knowing the detective in charge. Well, not knowing really. One was at Harvard with those bright, pushy Jews without having to know them. But he did recall Len Schwartz—athletics, gymnastics, quite a jock for a little chosen one. Must be unusual, ending up a policeman; the whole history he'd dredged from the data pools he was plugged into—interesting.

And the Horvay thing was going well. The data had

turned up something interesting, a hint that all mightn't have been so lily-white in Horvay's dealings. He'd have to find out more. Maybe then he'd ask Bobo, casually, of course.

He sat at the screen looking at the market data. Good. One way and another, he told himself, he'd made a killing.

11

"That gallery wasn't so special. The Met's bigger. The Frick's more elegant," Schwartz said, meeting Karen at the restaurant's small bar.

She kissed him. "Cute," she said, "Raymond Chandler."

Schwartz said, "Ha! You're supposed to read art history; I'm supposed to read detectives. Shall we sit? We have a booth." He picked up his drink and nodded Karen across the room. A woman took Karen's coat up a spiral staircase by the front window.

"We haven't been out to dinner for a long time, and now Raoul's. Is this a celebration?"

"Sure, why not? There's Ed, who's getting better. There's the weather—supposed to be in the fifties tomorrow. And there's both of us at the Sylvester Gallery today."

"I'm not complaining. I don't need any excuse; I'd even drink to it if—" Karen stopped, caught the waiter's eye and ordered a drink.

"Here's to coincidence and hunches," Schwartz proposed.

"Coincidence and hunches." Karen drank. "OK, I know the coincidence, but what's the hunch? Oh, wasn't Angela Sylvester wonderful-looking?"

"Yes. Don't confuse me. Besides, I'm starving, so let's order before it gets too busy in here. Red or white?"

"Oh, red. Let's order the food and some, uh, are we celebrating enough for a Clos de Vougeot?"

Schwartz nodded.

They ordered and talked about Ed, about how he was at home now and doing physio, about how he was sure the people who beat him were doing impossible stage faggot imitations, about how Schwartz was sure it was cops or set up by cops—by Gallagher, but why or for whom, he couldn't guess—about how useless it would be chasing that one down now.

Then the wine came and they thought they'd save it until hors d'oeuvres, but it tasted so good—they both tasted it; the waiter was told by Karen she'd taste it, too. So they were into the second glass when hors d'oeuvres came and Schwartz thought what the hell and Karen seconded the thought and caught a waitress's eye and tapped the bottle and moved her finger so that she'd bring another. And after all this she had Schwartz get down to his hunch.

He asked, "She say anything to you about Horvay's luck?"

95

"Yes. Extraordinary, all those finds."

"What do you make of it?"

"Well, I could follow them up with one of my contacts, but I'm inclined to accept it. The great dealers always seem to have the luck. But when you know, it's not really luck. They keep covering all possible sources and know what to look for, know how to look under, too. You know, under repainted surfaces, centuries of heavy revarnishings, cut-down canvases."

"Cut-down?"

"Sure. The nineteenth century decided symmetry was the thing so they cut or folded canvases to be perfectly centered. Mad—but they did it."

"All right. But let's suppose that I was a greedy dealer. An expert, successful enough but greedy. So I want to set up a swindle. Fakes. I have the selling outlets, of course, but what else would I need?"

Karen smiled and leaned in on an elbow, her chin in her hand. "I have to tell you quietly, Len, or else they'll all hear and everyone will be doing it. Well, first you'd need to find a rare person—a master painter. I mean one of unbelievable technical ability, and that's rarer than most would think in itself. But harder to find one without a personality to put in his own style. Or hers, though I don't know of any good woman forger."

"Wait. What do you mean?"

"Even the clever ones, like Van Meergeren, the Vermeer counterfeiter, put in his own style."

"Yeah, OK. But if you did have this great technician with no personality, couldn't you use the same technology you do to check for fakes to help create fakes?"

Karen nodded. "You're a clever detective. Yes. Yes, that's how," she said, her voice animated, speeding up.

And through the main course and into the second bottle of wine Karen told him how if you could get a range of x-rays of the work of the painter you wanted to fake, your master imitator could learn the brushwork, even the changing brushwork of different periods. And if you had the lab reports, the good faker or fake team could learn the pigment make-up. But care had to be taken; some otherwise good forgeries had fouled up over something elemental—like using zinc white to fake a painting earlier than mid-eighteenth century, since it was only invented then. And you could duplicate canvas types. Then you had all the considerations of wear and aging. Then, of course, getting the style and subject matter right, but that was the least of it. How, yes, if it were thoroughly set up, it just might work.

"Dessert or cheese or . . ."

"Let's have cheese to finish the wine," Karen said.

They had cheese. Raoul's was packed, noisy, warm. The wine was fuming nicely in Schwartz's head.

"So who would, I mean, besides Horvay and this magic painter, who would this setup need?" he asked.

"I don't think they could do it themselves, even though it's possible that someone like Horvay could get some of the scientific stuff. No, only the conservation labs of the museums, bigger ones at that, could provide the full range of technology. So your other person would be someone, say, someone from a museum with access to the labs, to getting or copying all they needed. And still—" Karen stopped.

"What?"

"No, it's just too improbable that anyone could be technically good enough to paint it. You'd almost need a team of two or three helping the painter with preparation. No."

"So"—Schwartz sighed—"you really don't think it's on? In theory, I mean."

"Of course, it's on in theory."

"But—"

"Because we're only talking about the technical basis. It's still the eye, the judgment of the expert eye, you see? So, if Horvay, or whoever, himself an expert, had someone on the team who was another great authority—"

"And in a museum, a likely place," Schwartz put in.

"Right," said Karen. "Well, it could be done. A long shot, but theoretically it's all possible. Are we having coffee here? Want to go somewhere else for coffee?"

Schwartz looked at Karen's flushed face. What a flush, what a face. He leaned way over the table. "You know what I'd like to do now? Come here."

Karen leaned towards him. Schwartz whispered over her cheek.

"Why, Len, that's absolutely obscene. Yes, please."

~~~~~~ 12

Peter Frascatti walked around the Met to staff parking. He surprised Billy, who turned off the radio, jumped out and opened the door for his boss. The trustees' meeting had ended earlier than planned.

Frascatti liked the meetings. He liked being a trustee. He liked paintings and was glad to be in a position to help. Over four million in the past three years, and two of those his own donation towards the Carpaccio. Not bad for a Jersey boy, son of a construction man who had started with nothing. And his father with that accent all his life, not to mention the old man's contacts.

Peter Frascatti kept his contacts with the rackets, the mob, whatever the papers liked to call it. He kept them at as long a distance as possible without seeming afraid or ashamed because you never knew when they'd be useful. Or how. The car came out of the park, going west.

Of course, you kept this a long, long distance from your art interests or from the Republican hierarchy in the city and Jersey. But funny how they'd meet. Like where he was going.

"An hour," he said to Billy, who'd turned off Bleecker and was slowing into a hydrant in front of the Small Bore Club.

He smiled going in. He always did, thinking of what his old man would think of his hobnobbing with the top cops, among others. He guessed the old fellow would have screamed, *"Cretino,"* taken a swipe at his head and finally appreciated it.

At the bar he said hello to an Albany big shot talking with young Sal.

"Hello, Sal. Working hard?"

"Always, Mr. Frascatti."

"Give my respects to your uncle Franco."

"Sure will. He asks after you."

"Listen," said the big shot, "this kid is really good on tax shelters."

Frascatti smiled. "He's one of the best lawyers in New York. See you around. Take care." And he walked off, thinking, Albany big shot—peanut vendor!

Later, twenty-five feet below, Frascatti was taking off his ear guards and checking the target cards in his hands. He gave them back to Johnnie Sheridan; Sheridan gave back his.

"I make that fifteen points I owe you," said Frascatti. "Not one of my better days."

"Bad luck, Peter. You've been within five or six

recently, and you drubbed me two weeks ago. Yes, I make it fifteen."

"I'll get you again, Johnnie."

They thumped each other's padded jacket and shook hands. Frascatti had just lost fifteen thousand dollars to Sheridan. He'd give him a check. What he regretted was the bad shooting—first-class compared to anyone's but Sheridan's. Smooth WASP prick.

On the way out he waved at him. Sheridan was by the message board, a card with the embossed seal of the Associazione Antica Romolo e Remo in his hand.

13

It seemed to Schwartz he was moving sideways on this. Not sideways like crabs—they knew where they were going. But sideways like being pushed a bit and going along a bit with a current of . . . Here he lost the metaphor. Warm water? Sewage? Screw the metaphor. Karen might see it as a return of his old "form," whatever that was. It didn't seem any good to him.

Well, let Karen get on with the art details; he'd keep sidling to corners. Like Horvay's tailors. Why the hell not? If Santini in his medical wisdom could try out his AIDS theory in the autopsy and that had come to nothing, a small anal cyst, a few unfriendly staphs around the prostate, well, why not Horvay's tailor?

Bob, of course, had worked out all the financial records, bank statements, had checked them with the firms Horvay'd done business with. All checked out.

Still, there was nothing like being in the victim's setting. Schwartz wasn't sure why there was nothing like it.

This came to him in the elevator going up to Hervey and Hervey's. Along with feeling self-conscious about his clothes. He never felt like this except when he went to buy clothes. He realized that what he liked about a place like Syms, besides the bargains, was the fact that there was no snotty salesman looking at your sports jacket as if it needed delousing. Besides—he took off his overcoat and looked down—there was nothing wrong here. Old, but Bloomie's best. Well, second best.

Anyhow, the hell with it. The elevator stopped and he went down to the door. If he looked a bit sloppy, it was what Karen told him was "Harvard Square sloppy." So there.

He opened the door and thought, oh-oh. A very well-dressed older man was standing by a table staring at him as if he were a plague rat. And he was probably the janitor.

"Yes, sir, and what can we do for you?" the man asked, somehow making it sound as if he meant "and what can we do *with* you?"

In a loud voice calculated to bring property values down, Schwartz said, "New York Police Department. Homicide investigation. Want to check the financial records of a murdered man. Customer of yours."

"This way, sir," the man said, his shoulders, as Schwartz saw them, giving an involuntary cringe, although it could have been a disclaimer shrug as they passed the few other people around.

103

Schwartz noted the nice wools and tweeds and thought maybe it wouldn't be a bad idea to get a lightweight wool for spring. OK, so it would be, what, three hundred?

"What?" he asked the accountant ten minutes later in a small, accounts-jammed office where only Bartleby the Scrivener could be at home. "Suits start at fourteen hundred dollars?"

"I know. Terrible, isn't it? But we can't keep up with the demand. We're at eight weeks now. Well, here it is. I thought it best to bring you the fitting book on Mr. Horvay. That would have everything, and here you see where each item begins and ends. And"—he turned a few pages—"here's the payment and dates. Much faster than our accounts books. Just call if you need me. I'm next door."

Working with the book and his pocket calculator, in the next ten minutes Schwartz found that Horvay's nineteen hundred dollars in check payments for the past year was correct. He also found that Horvay had bought a rag or two here for cash. Thirteen thousand, four hundred and thirty dollars' worth. And some change. He flipped the book back to the year before. Cash, cash, cash, cash. A suit for twenty-three hundred dollars? Jesus, thought Schwartz, he should've been shot just for that. Then he thought it wasn't a very professional observation. He closed the book, started drumming on the desk with his fingers and thinking. He thought of the contents of Horvay's apartment. Closets of good clothes but nothing like this. He thought of all that paid for in cash. Some sort of tax scam? Undeclared income? All the gallery accounts had checked out and the quick IRS check was all right. Some other source? Undeclared cash? What the hell did it mean?

He thought of his father schlepping all over trying to get very poor people to unionize for a living wage. Then he thought of this place and its twenty-three-hundred-dollar suits.

"Enough," he said out loud, got up and walked out, thanking the accountant in the next office. He found his way back to the entrance hall. And there, by the headless tailor's dummy, was the dandy he'd seen— Then he remembered him.

"Are you John Sheridan?"

"Yes." He looked down with a polite nod.

"Len Schwartz. We were at Harvard together."

"Well, yes, of course. You were the track star. I remember. Yes, Len. How are you?"

"Fine, fine." That very strong hand. "Ah, do you see any of the old . . . uh, our classmates?" Schwartz asked, remembering that they hadn't been in exactly the same crowd.

"Oh, a few, here in the city. You know, people I'd see anyway. But I don't go to the reunions. You?"

"I went to the twentieth last year. It was very strange. All those bald, white-haired, middle-aged wrecks. And the so obvious great successes. But that physical change was staggering."

"I know what you mean. Someone will say hello in the street and I stare and stare. Then he'll say he's Billy Philips, and I have to keep from saying, 'I don't believe it, how disgusting you've become!' But you certainly look in shape, Len."

"I try. But you, you're in shape. You really haven't changed at all since college."

"Odd we haven't bumped into each other here, before," said Sheridan. He said it as if he hadn't noticed Schwartz's clothes.

"You must be joking. I can't get clothes here. I'm just a workingman, John."

Sheridan smiled. "We're all workingmen, Len. What do you work at?"

"I'm a policeman, a detective."

"No? Really? Now, that's interesting. Good for you."

"Well, that's a refreshing reaction. In Cambridge last June it was all champagne, strawberries and scorn."

"I know. Like the reaction I get with some of them when they learn I was in the army in Vietnam. As if I were a criminal rather than just an ordinary person enabling them to be the liberal media stars, or whatever they are." Sheridan's voice kept the same half-amused slur throughout. "So you and I really do much the same."

"How's that?" Schwartz asked, grinning, feeling he probably wouldn't want to be put too close to the position of John Sheridan on Vietnam.

"Well, in different ways, but both doing something about old law and order. And even now I'm something of a detective. I try to figure out what's actually behind the stock market, what companies really are worth, rather than what they'd like to be worth."

"I see," Schwartz said, wondering if Sheridan wasn't too bright or was putting him on.

"Well, Len, good running into you again. Let's keep in touch, shall we? You still run?"

"Sure. Not as fast, but longer."

"Where?"

"Police gym in really bad weather, but mostly in Prospect Park, in Brooklyn, near where I live."

"Yes. I usually run in Central Park. Maybe we could meet in the warmer weather, May, whenever."

"Why not? Tell you what, John, why wait? Come on out to my place, say, Saturday morning, early. We'll run and then have breakfast; then, next time, I'll run in Central Park. Here, I'll give you my address."

"Yes. All right, good idea. I'll call to confirm. And here's mine," said Sheridan, handing Schwartz a card.

"Great," said Schwartz, "terrific running into you again."

Waiting for the elevator down, he wondered what all that had been about. Why did he bother to play those games? Sheridan wouldn't call. Why should Sheridan be interested in the company of a Jewish cop? Still, he wondered what Karen would think of this character if he ever did turn up.

~~~~~ 14

At seven on Saturday morning Schwartz stood on the steps of his Park Slope house telling Sheridan that yes, his car would be all right on that side of the street. He didn't bother asking if Sheridan's was the brown Bentley convertible. On the other hand, here was Sheridan turned up in old plain gray sweat gear rather than the *haute couture* joggies he would have bet on, so you never knew.

"We'll go up to the park, the top of the street. Then—what's good, about an hour?"

"Yes. That'd be fine, Len."

They jogged off, Sheridan remarking what a nice area, interesting town houses, nice scale and landscaping—talking, in fact, the way anyone might. Schwartz was surprised. They crossed Prospect Park West and went in.

"Know the park?" asked Schwartz.

"I recall being taken here as a child. But I don't remember. This is terrific."

They were coming down the rise into Long Meadow. Schwartz felt happy, as if it were his landscape. "Smaller than Central Park, but a great feeling because of no big buildings around. Originally all flat," he said, noting a stiffness in Sheridan's gait. "All the hills and dales are Olmsted's." Schwartz wondered if an hour would be way too much. Well, he'd see. He could always find a polite way, say he was bushed himself, and head back home.

They ran south over the wet grass. A morning mist came up waist-high on the meadow. A lighter mist hung from the sky. They passed hillside snow patches, thawing, outlined in dark earth. From time to time the ground went soft underfoot. Mud sucked, shot up in black-brown jets. They went over the top and down into the playing fields.

"Still have your HAA sweat shirt," said Sheridan as they passed the sodden softball diamonds.

"No, I cheated. I picked this up last year. My old ones wore out." Schwartz hoped John wouldn't tire himself by too much talk.

"You were very good. All-American or something?" Sheridan went on.

Schwartz laughed. "No. All Ivy League. That's like All-Brooklyn Little League. No," he added, "that's an insult to Brooklyn Little League."

They came up through trees and went over the hillcrest, down to the path beside the road and then left.

"How are you doing?" asked Schwartz.

"Fine. It's nice here. We've hardly passed anyone. By this time on the weekend Central Park is tied up in jogger jams. I don't see why half of them do it. Walking would be better for them. They're a dreadful lot," he said, laughing.

Well, he didn't seem to be tiring. If anything, Schwartz saw that the stiffness had gone from Sheridan's stride. All right then.

"Up here?" He nodded to a steep path on their left.

"Good," said Sheridan.

And up they went towards Nethermead. And then around the Nethermead path and down behind the boathouse and back south, Schwartz keeping them to the concrete until the path to Lookout Hill, then crossing up there, up the steps and over, taking them left through a steep trail, too slick now so that they had to take care and slipped and slid down to the roadside.

Then they came to the lake and ran around its curved inlets edged with the husks of last year's reeds. Mist rolled over them from the water. Sunlight began to break through.

Since they had come down the hill, their pace had increased. But Sheridan seemed all right, so Schwartz didn't slow it. Now they ran by the parking lot at Wollman Rink, then rejoined the path behind Nethermead and passed the Lefferts Homestead, behind the zoo, the ground rising and falling and then the other side of Long Meadow, beneath the Vale of Cashmere and turning up at the Grand Army Plaza end, making the first circuit a quarter of the way back down Long Meadow.

Too fast, Schwartz thought. He really should stop showing off but then thought, Why not? He didn't have the Bentley, the suits that cost thousands, the name, the swagger. But he had running. Why shouldn't this Harvard clubby be pushed a little?

"OK for another circuit? We can keep more out of the mud," Schwartz added for form.

"Fine," said Sheridan.

By the middle of the second circuit around Prospect Park, Schwartz had forgotten Sheridan and was beginning to enjoy the running, getting into a rhythm, feet, ankles, legs, thighs swinging easy from the hips, arms moving easy from the shoulders, breathing good and deep and slow.

At the end of that circuit he raised his eyebrows to Sheridan, who nodded and moved off at a faster pace. They'd been faster than a jog since a third way into the first circuit. Now Sheridan was going at it like a cross-country runner. What had his sport been? Football, wasn't it?

All right, Schwartz thought, let's go running, old sport. He kicked a bit, caught up with Sheridan and then, very slowly, very consciously kept pushing up the pace. The rhythm didn't leave him; he was too experienced a runner for that, but in the third circuit his attention kept moving to Sheridan, to how damned contained he was, as if . . . but Schwartz couldn't figure out what it was.

He didn't even bother looking at the end of the third. He kicked it, passed Sheridan quickly and heard himself thinking in the rhythm of his stride that She/ri/dan/was/all/grown/up/and/knew/his/way/through/Pros/pect/Park.

At the bottom of the lake path Sheridan came up alongside, looking . . . what the hell was it? There was no shortcut he could have taken, and Schwartz knew he hadn't slowed his pace.

They came around together by the parking lot. Something by Schwartz's ear. Bang! A milk bottle crashed beside them. Schwartz scarcely believed what he saw. In the instant of the sound Sheridan fell right, rolled over on the ground and rose sprinting in the same motion with an enormous animal roar. He took a dozen strides towards the four black ten-year-olds, who ran off, terrified, onto Ocean Avenue. Schwartz barely had time to turn to slow and run in place to witness this when Sheridan was back, laughing, running as if nothing had happened. Schwartz was a bit terrified himself—of Sheridan.

"Some performance," he said.

Sheridan smiled and said, "Oh, they're devils."

Schwartz heard him say "devils" not as it's said about nasty kids but as by a believer in devils.

"Oh, the roll. Yes, must seem strange. That's my army years. That's Vietnam. Come on, let's run," Sheridan said lightly, moving off still faster.

For the rest of the circuit and into the next, Schwartz hung ten yards back of Sheridan, thinking, finding his rhythm again.

Then, halfway down Long Meadow, the sun out bright, people walking about, he figured out what it was that puzzled him. That containment of Sheridan's— it was as if he fed off the energy he burned. It didn't make any physical sense, but there it was. As if terrific effort produced a nervous high that put more energy into him—for a time anyway.

112

Schwartz thought yes, he had enough left in him to test this out. At the road to the lake he came up alongside Sheridan, who nodded pleasantly. He slowed their pace, as a trained runner could without making it obvious. But it was still one killer pace. As they passed the boathouse, Schwartz lifted his chin.

"Up there—want to do some real cross-country?"

"Why not? Yes," answered Sheridan. "Lead the way."

Schwartz moved forward, readying himself, came to the fork in the path and jumped off between, into the part of the park called the Ravine. Down, down, wet leaves, down, pumping for momentum to go up, up, up, carrying up halfway and then pulling and letting his weight fall forward, hearing the crashing behind him. Sheridan.

Over the top and down the next, his advantage going down. Lighter than Sheridan and knowing the trail, he could let himself go more, Sheridan putting more into holding back to keep from falling.

But uphill behind him, Sheridan catching up, at five feet behind him like a jungle beast, a tank.

Once more down. Schwartz flew down and heard it, a sort of growl, knew Sheridan wasn't holding back and the trail too narrow here. Sheridan's noise, the heat of him and crashing off the trail, right through brush and stick brush and passing him and pulling out up the last hill rising over Long Meadow and another growl, grunt, whatever and Sheridan, god damn it, sprinting three hundred yards up the meadow and waiting for him, running in place at the top end.

Sheridan was smiling. "Terrific stuff." He nodded as Schwartz came up.

113

"Impressive." Schwartz smiled back, Sheridan picking up with him again.

"All right?" asked Sheridan, slowing at the end of the circuit.

Schwartz pretended he didn't hear it as a question and went down the meadow again with a slight grin.

This time he stuck to the trail and had a good rhythm back by the zoo, where Sheridan caught up with him.

"This is the last one," said Schwartz.

Sheridan nodded and, as Schwartz expected, went up on him thirty or forty yards.

By the time they rounded the top of Long Meadow, it was twenty yards; Schwartz kicked, came up and passed the unsmiling Sheridan, came out on the street a good sixty yards ahead of him and jogged in place, waiting.

"Great running, Len," Sheridan said as they crossed the avenue.

"Hmm. Well, I owe you an apology. I've been a runner all my life. I set you up."

"I know it. Don't apologize," said Sheridan as they ran down slowly towards Schwartz's house. "Winning is what it's all about. Does breakfast come with this?" he asked, smiling, steaming, looking towards the house, where Karen stood on the stoop watching them come towards her.

～～～ 15

Under the shower in the top bathroom Schwartz felt the nausea rise in his stomach like a greasy wave. He turned the tap hotter. His head still ached; the veins throbbed above his ears. Some run. It must have been eight miles, no, more like ten. And what he'd had to do to beat Sheridan. What an animal. Literally, he meant. Some sort of big cat. That business with the bottle and then crashing through the ravine and *then* sprinting flat out, and then and then.

The nausea passed. Sheridan—the run hardly showed. He was breathing deep, downstairs, that's all. A bit flushed with exercise. Jesus, and he isn't even a runner. Schwartz wondered what he'd done in Vietnam. Then he thought he didn't want to know. Big, yes. But who'd think, looking at him, the ordinary sort of . . . No. Wait. The way Karen looked at him when he'd introduced them. What, flirty? No. Not really, more like how she'd look at a painting—something new she sees that fascinates her.

Schwartz went down to breakfast. Karen and Sheridan were sitting at the dining-room table, sipping orange juice.

"I've been telling Karen how nice I find the park and this whole area. And she's been telling me about its history. Fascinating, like this house."

Schwartz sat, poured orange juice and drank it down.

"This room's a good example," Karen said. "The architect obviously couldn't decide whether he liked Beaux Arts or Art Nouveau, so he mixed them. And then the oriel window, thrown in for good luck."

"And," said Schwartz, taking coffee, "to impress his clients with his superior education."

"Who would they have been?" Sheridan asked.

"People like us," said Karen.

Sheridan nodded.

"People like *us,*" said Schwartz, looking at Sheridan's knockabout cashmere sports jacket and scratching at his elbow through the hole in his sweater.

"Was this a Jewish neighborhood then?"

"No," Karen said, "it was German, Scottish and English. The churches around are, or were, mostly Lutheran, Episcopal, Presbyterian." She passed scrambled eggs.

"John," said Schwartz, "when I said 'us,' I didn't mean us," sweeping his arm. "I meant us," swinging his arm between Karen and himself. "And as you now know, even that 'us' would be more accurately thought

116

of as *this* us," opening his hand towards Karen, then finding that he needed to stroke her arm.

They all laughed. Karen touched Schwartz's hand. He was glad. She kept looking at Sheridan. Sheridan passed the plate of smoked fish to Schwartz. Schwartz noted that Sheridan looked comfortable with a bagel.

"What's your field, John?" Karen asked.

Schwartz moved his ankle until it touched Karen's instep.

"Oh, I'm one of those dull Wall Street types—even duller, I suppose, since with computers I can pretty much operate from home."

Karen said, "I'll bet that's not really dull."

Schwartz slid his foot up Karen's calf. She moved it away.

"It is. It really is dull. But it's one's living, so one does it as well as possible. Now you two, those are fascinating jobs. A detective and—I suppose an art historian is another kind of detective." Sheridan ended looking at Karen as if he'd said something very different from this conversational pleasantry.

"Yes, but great stretches of it can be, well, if not dull, then very, very slow. Lord, yes!" She laughed. "Oh, years slow."

Schwartz looked at Karen, then glanced at Sheridan looking at Karen. "Me, too. Most police work is dull. Matter of sifting and sifting through so much you know is going to be irrelevant. But you keep at it. A statistical business, really. Success through attrition mostly." Schwartz stopped, feeling so like making love to Karen that he forgot what he'd just said.

"What's your specialty? If police detectives have

them, I mean," Sheridan added, glancing at Schwartz between looking at Karen.

Karen was looking at both of them. Schwartz wondered how she could be so unselfconscious, so . . . beautiful.

"Huh?" Schwartz said, seeing both Karen and Sheridan look at him. "Oh. Uh, homicide mostly. Dull enough. Like what I was doing when I bumped into you, John. Jesus, checking tailor accounts. Oh, did you know this art dealer Alex Horvay?"

"Yes. I met him at openings. A few times at his gallery, a few times at the Met. Awful, his being killed like that. He was charming and, of course, a fine dealer. A real authority. But of course, you know all this."

"Yup. That's what I mean. I have to keep asking the same questions. I can ask five thousand times and still end up knowing no more than anyone who's read the papers."

"Still, of the three," Karen said, "maybe Len's job can be the least dull or slow since so much of it involves other people."

And on it went, the small talk, with Schwartz touching Karen at any opportunity, looking at her, thinking of her when he wasn't looking at her, growing more and more excited.

Finally, with some vague promise for a return run in Central Park, Sheridan was off, shaking hands in a way Schwartz found slightly irritating, the handshake of a god descended.

"And now," Schwartz said, turning to Karen after the front door shut.

"He's amazing."

"What? What do you mean, amazing? Just because he's six-four, strong as steel, from an old aristocratic family, unbelievably wealthy, erudite . . . but does he have the interesting face I do? Huh? Does he have these dark eyes, darker rings beneath them . . . ?" He pulled Karen to him. "This interesting long nose, this amazingly interesting long . . ." He placed Karen's hand along the top of his thigh.

She pushed him away, laughing. "Oh, you cops. Ain't you got no class? Ain't you got no couth?" She turned and walked towards the stairs.

"What are you trying to say, Karen?"

She turned. "Are we going to stand gabbing in the hall all day, or are you going to come upstairs and fuck me?"

16

Len was downstairs reading one of the books on art forgeries she'd gotten for him. She couldn't even think about it in Len's presence. She adored Len. He was such a lover. He could be. Like just now. They'd both been so excited.

Still, there was nothing wrong with fantasy. She'd thought about both of them, John Sheridan and Len, both times, coming both times. Len was there, but so, somewhere, was John Sheridan. He'd tied her down, he'd . . .

They talked about their fantasies with each other. It excited them; it was a bond. Nothing wrong with that. But not this time she hadn't. So what? Other times, too, she hadn't. But not this time.

She shut her eyes. It was no fantasy. Len had been upstairs showering. She'd remembered there weren't clean towels in their bathroom and called in to John if it was all right to bring them in, and he'd answered yes, and she'd opened the door to see him naked, beautiful, glistening with sweat. And those eyes. And she hadn't been able to move, nonsense, hadn't wanted to, stood there feeling the heat come to her cheeks, feeling half-faint, fascinated, hypnotized, dumbstruck. And John Sheridan had taken the towels and her with them into his arms, and he was so tall, her face in the blond hair of his chest, belly. She could still imagine the smell of him. And he'd held her there, silent, not doing anything but holding her. She'd trembled. She wanted to kiss his body all over, but her mouth had trembled so, and the trembling ran through her into her womb. And he'd taken the towels and let her go, and she'd backed out of her own bathroom, trembling.

Karen smiled, remembering backing out of a room as if in the presence of royalty. What fantasy! That's all it was. He was a wonderful-looking thing. Those eyes. Nothing had happened. Nothing would. Just fantasy, the memory of what had happened. The fantasy was what had and what hadn't happened. She adored Len. Had always, except that once, those years ago, always kept the others just a fantasy. John Sheridan was just a fantasy. But she knew she wouldn't tell this fantasy to Len.

BOOK III

—————— **1**

When Sal suggested the gun club, Uncle Franco said no, as usual. He didn't like it. Too many Jew and Irish politicians, too many cops, too many "them damned English bankers," meaning everyone else. Sal, as usual, couldn't resist pointing out that a lot of those politicians, cops and bankers were Italian.

Uncle Franco didn't hear. He went on. "What'sa matter, Associazione Antica Romolo e Remo isn't good enough?"

"Yes, it's good enough." He imagined his uncle struggling to stand to attention as he said his club's name.

"It wasn't good to me?"

"Yes, yes, it was."

"It wasn't good to you, Salvatore?"

"Yes. Yes, Uncle Franco. It was very good to me. I'll pick you up, I'll take you there."

"Arright," came Uncle Franco's growl from the phone.

"Uncle Franco, I love you."

"I love you, Salvatore. You're a good boy."

The next day at two in the afternoon Sal drove his blue BMW cautiously down Mott Street.

"Are you all right back there, Uncle Franco?" In the mirror Sal saw the old man propped stiffly against the back seat, pushing on his cane.

"I'm OK. You just look after your nice new car."

Sal was trying to, but the torn-up street, part dirt, part steel plate and the rest cracked concrete, wasn't making it easy. "Jesus, what a mess they're making here. And look at the new condos. Completely against the zoning."

The end of the cane tapped on the seat back beside him. "Never mind zoning. Zoning. I'm gonna do well from what's going on these streets."

Sal smiled into the mirror. "So why aren't I your lawyer on this one?"

"You? Naw. Is not for you. My Joseph's doin' it."

They stopped behind a truck parked in the middle of the street. A teen-age boy crossed in front of them. His head was shaved except for a line of hair over the middle standing out in eight-inch pink spikes.

"Look at that," said Uncle Franco. "You could spit at it. These kids, you know what they don't have? Parents. They got pisspots for parents. If that was my kid—ah, what's the use? Listen"—tapping again with the cane—"you know why you're not in on this development, Salvatore? Is tricky business. Maybe, like you say, the zoning, maybe other things could be risky. My

Joseph's OK. But you, you're our *pietra preziosa*. You know?"

Sal shifted in his seat and drove. Here came the "jewel" speech.

"Jewel, that's what it means. Every family needs to have its jewel. You're our *pietra preziosa*, the jewel in the family crown. It's good for everyone you should be. You hear me? Salvatore? And don't be ashamed of it!"

"Here's the club, Uncle." Sal stopped in the street, got out and opened the rear door. A taxi honked behind them; neither of them bothered to look.

The club was a dark storefront with L'ASSOCIAZIONE ANTICA ROMOLO E REMO in neat white lettering on the window. On either side were painted crossed, small Italian and American flags. Beneath, in small print, it read PRIVATE—MEMBERS ONLY. The door had a green shade pulled part way down its half glass. There were a few plants on the window, nice plants, palms, if you looked hard, but it was hard to look in.

"OK," said Uncle Franco, up now and helped to the sidewalk, "I'm OK from here."

He tapped Sal's cheek with his hand. "Thanks. You pick me up around five. Yeah, five. That way I can have a little nap before dinner."

The cabby had stopped honking and lay slumped on his wheel as if dead. Sal thought of saying something but didn't, got in his car and drove downtown thinking what a strange old guy his uncle was and how much he loved him.

Old Franco stood in the street for a while, looking,

breathing it in, taking the old bearings. He squinted. Was that what's her name, the old lady from across the street? Not sure. The grocery. The bakery. More Chinamen, but there had always been some. Fewer Italians. Well, well, times change. He drew himself up. Still a big man. The wind flapped the gray coat on his frame. Seventy-eight years old, he thought, seeing his reflection in the door glass, and still a tall man, still straight. He went into his club. They'd make a fuss. They'd better.

At three-thirty this one comes into the club and is shown back into the meeting room "for club officials only." Big, maybe even taller than Franco used to be. *Molto elegante.* He wants to be called John Buxton. That's all right, too. People have their names, their reasons. And polite. This one always calls him sir, doesn't sit without an invitation. That's good. But Franco knew it was more than respect. He was no fool. This was an aristocrat, never mind that bullshit about no aristocrats in America. Connected with the owners, the ones who still owned it. Well, all right, he only wanted his share. Hadn't done badly. But not easy. Not like for this "Buxton."

But something else, not the respect for this Yankee *marchese, duca.* This one was a fox, a bull, a lion. Yes, and so was he when he was young. But not like this. This one was crazy, cold, not human, not even *uno bruto.* What? Like one of these machines. A computer where the heart should be. Sure. Old Franco's not stupid; of this one, he's afraid.

"So, Mr. Buxton," he said, the envelope in his hand, "this is from that friend of a friend that I don't know. And it's to finish the business and the terms are as before."

"Naturally."

"Naturally." Old Franco smiled, the aquiline nose still handsome, but the teeth not his. He put the envelope on the table between them without letting go of it.

"There's one difference, I'm told. It's not here. Not in America. That's all I know. So, what do you say, Mr. Buxton?"

"Perfectly all right, sir."

He dropped the end of the envelope. The other one picked it up and put it into the inner pocket of his suit jacket.

"A beautiful suit. I know a little something about clothing, Mr. Buxton, and you got a beautiful suit there."

"Thank you, sir. I think so. Nice of you to say it." He stood and draped his topcoat over his arm. "No, sir, please don't bother. It's been good seeing you. You're really looking very well."

"Well, I'm an old man, but I try. Bye-bye."

"Good-bye, sir," he said, shutting the door.

Old Franco waited. He heard the street door buzzer go off twice. Then he shouted, "Monty, Monty, *un espresso,* a double, *subito!*"

He moved in the chair as if trying to shake something off himself. No, he thought, it's not just that you're old, Franco. That one'd give anyone the creeps.

~~~~~~ **2**

Afterwards, until the phone rang, Schwartz went into one of his reverie debates with his dead father. This one went:

"You see, Dad, that was Don Phillips, New York City chief of detectives. Only the commissioner is higher. And Don Phillips is black. You see that?"

And then the remembered voice, hard, flat: "So?"

"No, not just a token, like you're thinking."

"Who was thinking token?"

"Look, Dad, sure he's had to compromise, not make enemies, but he's also had to be a fine cop, a good manager, twice as good as a white man to get there. He's sort of a hero to me."

Then the flat "He's a sellout. To his race, his class."

Then the voice—there was hardly an image—turned and left, and Schwartz was left feeling more alone than when he started. He wanted to call him back. It was important that his father explain—

The phone rang.

"Yes. Yes, Tom, the chief was just here. . . . What do you mean? You know what he wanted. But I insisted that he keep you on for a while longer. Then, if you're still screwing up, I'd consider taking your job. . . . All right, seriously. The chief of detectives just happens to drop in. All right, so he's known for these impromptu visits on his staff. And two minutes after he leaves you're calling me from the other side of the plaza asking what he wanted? . . . No. Pull the other one, Tom. Why not just bug my office, tap my phone, or am I after the fact? . . . Damn right. It's not your style. . . . OK, as if you didn't know, he was his usual nice self. Courtly even. Glad to have me back 'in the middle of things again,' was how he put it. Appreciated the trickiness of the case. Thought it was seeming less likely connected with West Side gay clubs. And he was happy—did you hear that, Tom?—happy about it . . . for the obvious political reasons. . . . No, ask someone else. So then we talked a bit about Brooklyn, our families. You know. OK. . . . I will, Tom. You take care, too."

Schwartz put the phone down, kept looking at it and began to tap the table.

"Ahem."

He looked up at Bob, hovering diffidently.

"Gallagher is driving me crazy with his watching and listening."

"I know, I heard. Uh, you were talking loud, I mean. I've some, well, I hope good news. You know

131

how you said to check other places where Horvay bought stuff? Well, it was the same. A bundle paid in cash, like at his tailors. So then I ran through his tax records and checked that against his own books—and there was something funny going on. Looks like swindling the IRS, at least."

"And his accountants?"

"A business accountant, yes. But he did his own taxes."

"Let's get it clear. Is this cash spending of unaccounted income or is it Horvay's accountable income that he wasn't declaring?"

"About a quarter is unaccounted; most he just didn't declare. He was lucky to get away with it. We checked—no IRS case was pending."

"Lucky." Schwartz's table tapping grew fainter, stopped. He flipped through a file on his desk labeled "Art News." "Bob, when did this start?"

Bob looked at a notebook. "Early seventies. Uh, seventy-three. Len."

Schwartz smiled. "Well, we just might be on to something. Good work, Bob. Terrific, really. Relax, call me sir."

~~~~~~ **3**

On a springlike Wednesday in an early April which had so far set records for cold, Schwartz sat on a bench looking at the geometries of the Met extensions south and west into the park. Carrots, celery, bananas. A training lunch after the run and gym workout that morning. Schwartz was always in some sort of training, but this was a bit much, even for him. What it was for, he couldn't exactly say. Another "friendly" run was coming up, on Sheridan's turf this time, but it wasn't only that. He wasn't even a physical cop; detective inspectors were supposed to be—not intellectual, not that for sure—steady, thinking bureaucrats, sorting through, slowly, methodically sorting. . . . The new wings of the Met made nice patterns. . . .

A very white and black woman walked by . . . nice patterns those—were they tetrahedrons?

They were very white legs from out a black trench coat that had come back into his vision.

"Inspector Schwartz, is it?"

He looked up. A beauty. He started to rise.

"Don't get up. You don't remember. I'm Angela Sylvester, from the gallery."

"Of course," he said, standing, his open briefcase in his arms like a shopping basket, with celery sticking out. He could think of nothing sensible to say. A number of very nonsensical things, but nothing sensible.

"You seem very busy," she said, smiling towards the celery.

"Oh, yeah. This. Well, it's a new secret sound device I'm testing for the department." He broke a piece off and ate it. "Yes, that's it. I hear much better now. Sit down, won't you?"

She sat on the bench.

"Well," she said.

"Well," he said, thinking that she was wonderful-looking and, almost simultaneously, that he was acting like some teen-age schmuck.

"How's the investigation going?" She turned towards him conversationally, her crossed legs swinging in to the edge of the bench.

Those legs. What was it he was reminded of; what had he thought? Pearl? No. Ivory? No. "Alabaster."

"Alabaster, Inspector?"

"No, no. I didn't say . . . Maybe you need one of these," he said, offering a stick of celery.

She shook her head, laughed, looked down at her legs and quietly said, "Oh, alabaster." She kept her eyes down.

Schwartz wanted to crawl into his briefcase, but there was no relief in there. In there a banana winked at him. Schwartz knew he wasn't crazy: he didn't wink back.

They looked up at the same time and for a second saw it in each other's eyes. Schwartz looked up to the building's angles.

"You're a strange policeman. I mean, I don't mean . . . I mean. You're silly. I like you."

Schwartz, the aging athlete, felt his heart beat. He looked at the celery. "Everything you say will be digested." He looked at Angela.

She was looking at him steadily. "I'm aware of my rights."

"Right," he said, "then I have to ask . . . those dark eyebrows and black lashes?"

"A bit of outside help, I admit, but basically they're mine."

"And I suppose you have a permit for your eyes?"

"I didn't think they were an offensive weapon."

"Not in the least. But dangerous"—he looked down— "like alabaster."

"Alabaster? Oh, alabaster's an invasion of privacy. After all, what would you say if I asked you about your . . . body, Inspector?"

"I'd have to warn you it could be held against you," he said, looking up again. "But you could plead"—he waved his hand—"the first day of spring, the wind, the general craziness. Like there, that woodland creature."

They looked up the walk to where a stunted old man moved towards them with the rolling gait of a dwarf. Extraordinary. Up he swung in a light fawn coat and blue bowler hat.

And closer, like something sent by Pan. A gargoyle dressed by F. Tripler. Schwartz put out his hand to take Angela's.

The little man stopped.

"Inspector Schwartz, my husband, David Sylvester."

—————— **4**

"**H**orvay," she said, touching the coat arm gently.

"Ah, yes. Angela told me about you. Very impressed. I was away, you see. If there's any way I can help . . ." Sylvester said in a musical bass.

Schwartz heard the sounds; the content could have been Albanian for all he understood, half standing, half crouching so that maybe he'd be invisible. Then he thought Sylvester would see the posture as condescending, but the effort to straighten was matched by an equal pull to disappear.

"Please, sit," said Sylvester, tactfully.

"No. Nice meeting you, sir. I have to go," Schwartz improvised, and bemoaned that "sir." Sylvester must think him . . .

"A detective. Interesting, in that I do detective work hunting for paintings. I'm known as a great snoop.

137

Shall we walk on together? Of course," he said, "I'm obviously no master of disguise." He gave a perfectly genuine smile saying this.

Angela took his arm. Schwartz took a breath. They walked.

"And if I may ask, is the case coming along?" came the rich, low voice.

"Not so anybody'd notice. But sometimes it's a matter of eliminating alternatives. I wonder . . . Let me put it this way, Mr. Sylvester: Would you have a conflict of interest in answering questions about Horvay's business dealings?"

A low laugh. "Certainly. When he was living. But he's . . . ceased being a competitor." Another laugh. "That makes me a suspect, doesn't it?"

"Of course not. But did you and Horvay ever go after the same paintings?"

"Yes, often. Well, a dozen, twenty times over the years."

"Who won? If that's not too crude a way of putting it."

"Well—" Sylvester began, and hesitated.

"David's too modest, Inspector. Up until six or seven years ago he did, we did, more often than Horvay. But then—not to speak ill, et cetera."

"You're very loyal, darling. But the truth is that it's a business like any other, Inspector Schwartz. Horvay was coming up with one sensational discovery after another, so he naturally developed a preeminent reputation in the field. Sellers and buyers thought first of him. Really as simple as that."

"And what did you think of his discoveries?"

138

"Ah, that's another question. Well, putting aside the envy—or is it jealousy? I'm always confusing them—no, I think I was, as you can imagine, professionally very curious. Oh, there are some dealers and curators who are better than others at finding the lost—that is, the undocumented—pieces. But Horvay was doing it at a, well, surprising rate. So I—and, I may add, the entire profession—made enough fuss, in our genteel, backstage way, of course, so that those paintings received extremely thorough scrutiny. And they all passed it."

"Unanimously?"

"No. This is art, not, say, car manufacture. But overwhelmingly. And at an atypically high level of technology as well. They were x-rayed, chemically analyzed—the works, Inspector. Some were even at the conservation department right here," he said, pointing to the Met through the still-unbudded trees.

Schwartz stopped, picked up a twig and rolled it between his fingers. "So is that your opinion? I didn't quite catch it."

"You didn't, quite," said Angela lightly, standing between them.

"No, it's not; not for most of them. It's not," Sylvester said in a quiet tone of voice, suggesting he really didn't like saying it.

"Even with x-rays and all the other?" Schwartz asked even more quietly, as if asking himself.

"The eye, Inspector. Finally, in these matters, it comes down to the eye."

"And what did your eye see that was wrong?"

"Nothing. Everything was perfect. Maybe that was

it. No surprises; the inevitably unpredictable wasn't there. Well, maybe it can't be put into words. But something in them didn't sit right for me. I never saw them enough, of course, but as much as I could, those paintings never grew for me. Do you know what I mean?"

Schwartz said, "The way you can keep seeing more and how what you've already seen deepens, grows more beautiful . . ." looking from little David Sylvester to his wife.

"Exactly. Yes. Well, my eye says, 'Not really,' to many of Horvay's great finds. But this sometimes happens. It's the nature of attribution."

"I see." Schwartz snapped open his briefcase, dug behind the celery and banana through some lined yellow legal paper, said, "Just a second, something . . ." dug some more and finally came up with a sheet he handed to Angela. "Look at this list I made. Do me a favor, describe it, categorize it, if you can."

Angela looked at Schwartz, then back at the list, which she held so that Sylvester could look on. She said, "Collectors, well known, a name here I don't know."

"I do," said Sylvester. "In Cleveland."

Angela continued. "Chicago and two new museums in Texas."

"This is what?" asked Sylvester. "A list of the buyers? I remember Chicago."

"That's right. Um, those well-known collectors—what do they collect specially?"

Angela leaned over the list again. It was at Sylvester's eye level.

"Fairchild—a bit of everything European. Seventeenth, eighteenth, nineteenth centuries," she said.

"Cohen, the same—some Impressionists, too," Sylvester said, looking down the list and then at his wife and then at Schwartz. A smile came across his face. "I see, Inspector."

"What do you see, Mr. Sylvester?"

"I see you're a detective. These are collectors and collections, but nothing that specializes in the provenance or period of those paintings. No great authorities here."

Schwartz put up a finger. "Except the Chicago Museum. I don't understand that."

Sylvester's finger went up and he smiled. "Ah, but I do. Chicago bought the Hobbema around ten years ago. And that was the only Horvay 'discovery' I thought good."

"Well, well," said Schwartz.

"Well, well," said Angela.

"Inspector—" Sylvester began.

"Len," said Schwartz.

"Len, you're clever. But in a lifetime you'd never prove this."

"But you'd make a statement. . . ."

"Of course, but I'm already on record. Look, I'm not trying to tell you your business. Mine is a good opinion, but in this case a minority against other good opinion. And since the others won't change their opinions, well . . . Besides, you can't expect much help from collectors who really aren't interested in the paintings they bought for millions becoming worth thousands."

141

Schwartz's smile had gone. "And I suppose the experts wouldn't . . ."

Sylvester looked at Angela. They shook their heads.

"No," said Angela, "they have reputations to maintain, and most of them have egos bigger than their reputations. And that one alone"—she pointed back towards the Met—"would stop you dead. Gerald Vandevelde. His reputation *is* as big as his ego."

"I've heard of him," Schwartz said.

"Chairman of European Painting. Very capable. Brilliant. While I have disagreed with him," Sylvester said in his Chaliapin voice, "I have the utmost respect for his judgment."

"Above reproach," Schwartz said flatly.

"No. I didn't say that. There was too much coincidence for me in those Horvay finds, and I never felt Vandevelde considered that enough."

"What coincidence?"

"For one, most of the works had no history—no mention of them, you understand? And the others had only been referred to, ambiguously, but had disappeared for one, two hundred years. And then the Wartena business. No, each on its own, quite possible. All together—let's say, less possible."

Schwartz stopped walking and frowned. "Wartena—I saw the name in one of the clippings."

"Baron Wartena, a major Dutch collector. Four of the paintings, the story goes, turned up buried on one of his farms. They'd been quickly hidden against the German invasion. Records were lost; the people who buried them died in the war—that sort of thing. And all so conveniently part of a collection always in his family since they were painted. Four or five, I remember, in six years. Almost one a year. Reclusive collector and all. Too much of a wonderfully good thing, I think. If you had time, Len, I could tell you more at the gallery. I have files on the major collectors. Part of my business."

"Yes, I can drive you over. The car's right there." Schwartz pointed through the trees, across a road to where the car was pulled up near the bridle path.

They looked at him.

"Part of my business. Outrageous parking rights."

The black earth smelled rich. Angela in the middle, the three walked under a clear blue sky, out of which Sylvester said, "I'd like you to call me David. My father changed his name from Silverstein to Sylvester. He was a furrier, though why he thought Sylvester would be a better name in that business I don't know. The rest of the family hated him for it. So out of a perverse loyalty to his memory or a loyalty to his perverse name changing, I keep the name. My parents were people of ordinary height and looks. I have two physically normal sisters. But I've been very lucky. My parents adored me and gave me everything, so I had confidence. God knows what it would have been like if I'd been born a girl. I work very hard."

They walked on. Schwartz could think of nothing to say. As they walked, Angela kept taking Schwartz's hand quite openly. He kept snatching it back, thinking she was insane.

Then David Sylvester continued. "Did you find the gallery pretentious? Don't answer. I love it. It's a workplace, a museum, a place of love for me—for us.

143

I'm very lucky, you see. I work, we work very hard, we make a good living. I'm loved by a wonderful, beautiful woman who's my very best friend. I adore her. She's my real happiness, Len. You find us a strange couple? Don't answer. I know my strengths; I know my more obvious limitations. I try not to be a fool. I love Angela; I don't own her. Her happiness is my happiness. Do you understand me, Len? What she wants, I want for her, and I'm a happy man."

"And I'm a happy woman," Angela said, bending and kissing her husband's cheek. "And I want you, Len," she continued quietly but well within David's hearing, and she squeezed Schwartz's hand.

And Schwartz would probably have been more embarrassed if the craziness hadn't made him so sexually excited. And even as he thought it, it sounded silly to him, but he thought, On this case, I need all the friends I can get.

5

Something had come up; John Sheridan had called to put the great Central Park rerun off for a week or so. He'd call Len to make a new date. Definitely. He wasn't letting him off the hook.

"The postponement of dubious pleasure—" Schwartz began. It seemed the first or second half of an epigram he couldn't complete, except for "is a dubious pleasure," which didn't exactly put him in La Rochefoucauld's league and which got him thinking of Angela Sylvester. But so, he realized, did shoelaces, trees, bits of paper or anything these days, including Karen. If he told Karen about this, he'd be all right. Nothing would happen then. He'd tell Karen.

But first he'd tell Gallagher. Not about Angela, about the picture that was emerging. Or staying in the shadow, in bits. Lots of little pictures, at least ten, as part of it.

145

Gallagher listened, after his fashion. His feet were up on his desk, a good sign.

"Go on, Lenny."

"But imagine, Tom, the whole scam worked *backwards*, for once. A couple of great authorities planning it—battle's half-won already. Getting all the technical stuff, hardware, having access to it. Then feeding it to this master forger or forgery team."

"Go on."

"And not just that, but over in Europe the setup with an eminently respectable front, the great collector."

"Go on."

"That's it. Don't you see? Then the masterminds are the two final authorities! Gutsy but theoretically airtight. Well?"

"Go on!" Gallagher said, laughing. "Look, Lenny," he said, pulling his feet off and bringing his chair up to the desk, covered with copies of Schwartz's notes, charts, lists, "I'm not saying you don't have anything here. You do."

"But it's all circumstantial, right?"

"That's it. And even so, putting that act together— that's elaborate. And, nothing personal, are you telling me that four—at least four—of them arty types are going to hang in there quiet as clams? Go on!" Gallagher made as if to push the notes aside.

"Tom, that's my point, too. They couldn't. Horvay gets greedy—we know that much—and he wants more, a bigger cut, a faster manufacture, whatever. And when the others can't talk him out of it, they shoot him out of it. Or he's getting too high-profile, so they decide he's too risky to have around. So they take out

a first-class contract. That fits, too. They're high rollers, and a big pot's at stake. Oh, Christ, Tom, you
know there's nothing in that gay passion theory!"

"All right, suppose the faggots didn't get him. What
you're peddling is still circumstantial, every bit of it. I
admit it's a terrific story, Lenny, but there's not a
hope of a case in it. For example"— he dropped his
voice—"if it's not too simple of me to point this out,
all this hasn't gotten us a hint of the killer." Gallagher's
voice rose. "And that's the crime. This is a murder
case, not an international art fraud case, Jesus Christ!"

"Now you're talking, Tom. I mean, shouting. That's
the Gallagher we all know and love," said Schwartz,
placing himself on a corner of the desk and putting
one arm across to Gallagher's thick shoulder. "You
clever bastard, Tom, you took the words right out of
my mouth. Make it an international art fraud case—
unofficially if that's best."

"What?" Gallagher squinted.

"So, first, I'll need your authority to go to Holland.
A week should do it."

"What?" Gallagher pushed Schwartz's hand off his
shoulder.

"Don't worry, whatever's necessary, we can work it
out with the Dutch police, Interpol, NATO. No
problem."

"What?" Gallagher stood up, walked around, went
back to his desk and fished out a big cheap cigar.

"Hey, I thought you quit. You know they're bad for
you."

"Shuddup."

"Not just your health, Boss, but well, the old im-

147

age, you know. Upwardly mobile cops just aren't seen chomping the El Ropos these days. No-no."

Gallagher took the cigar in his hands, twirled it, snapped it in two and dropped it into the wastebasket. "There, you moral little turd."

"I knew you'd thank me. Well, Boss?"

"All right, but no trip. First you use Interpol. Then, if you have to—we'll see. I'm not unreasonable. I'm not trying to screw you on this—as you so loyally thought I was."

"Who, me?" Schwartz asked, smiling.

"Just one thing about all this is fishy."

"What's that, Tom?"

"How come it coincides with all those tulips?"

"Tom, I never . . . but you're right. It's a great time to go."

6

No, Karen hadn't met David Sylvester. Why did Len keep telling her how nice he was "despite" that first impression of his deformity? And not a word about the wife—that cool marble beauty.

Yes, Karen was excited about the idea of going to Holland with Len. She even thought most of it could be underwritten as a publicity tour by her English and continental publishers since the book was soon to come out there. Yes, but why did he keep mixing this possible trip in with lists of David Sylvester's qualities? And why qualities "despite" his age and physical limitations? And nothing of ravishing Angela Sylvester.

Now he was on tulips. Tulips, for Christ's sake!

"You're smitten, aren't you?"

Schwartz stopped in mid-eulogy. "Smitten? With tulips? Is that the Dutch for tulipomania?"

His hyper side usually amused her. Not now.

"No. *Smitten* is a slightly old-fashioned, slightly euphemistic word meaning 'hot for Angela Sylvester.' "

"Ahh," he said. Then: "Ahhh?" Then he settled for "Ahh."

"Eloquently put, Leonard." She was angry despite the smile that wanted to come, seeing him look so like the dog caught with the Thanksgiving turkey in its mouth.

He saw her smile and, thankful as that dog, crossed to the sofa and sat by her. She picked his arm off her shoulder.

"Uh-uh. A little talk, please."

"Nothing's happened. Yes. I find her terrifically attractive. Don't you?"

"Oh, yes. But—not to seem puritanical—probably not to the same ends as you."

"Nothing's happened. I mean, one can be taken with somebody without . . ."

"Taking some body?"

"Yes, yes! Damn it, darling, don't tell me you weren't a bit smitten or tuliped by old John Sheridan?"

"Len, you're changing the subject."

"No. You found him attractive—I saw that. Jesus, almost twenty years together; there are some things we don't have to write each other memos about. But I know nothing happened with you and him. And nothing will. So it's the same with my . . . 'crush' on Angela."

Karen let his arm come up on her shoulder.

"I see the similarity in theory. But the practicality— the situations aren't at all alike. I met John once. You seem to be spending half your professional time—for the highest of motives, I'm sure—with her in that palazzo of a gallery."

"Not just her—" Schwartz began.

"Oh, yes, the old bent dwarf, he of all the 'limitations.' No doubt he's watching through a one-way mirror-window," she said, letting him rub her hair across the back of her neck.

They fell silent. His hand rubbed her hair. She heard his quiet breathing and the silence moved, tingled the flesh on the back of her arms under the soft brown sweater. Her hand moved onto the inside of his thigh.

"Besides," she said in a different voice, "it just so happens that John Sheridan is going with a, well, a professional acquaintance, actually one of my contacts in my snooping for you."

"Oh?" Schwartz asked, turning himself and holding Karen in both arms. "Who's that?"

"Georgia Morris. She's in European Painting at the Met. Oh, but she's very discreet, so don't be worried."

"Mmm," said Schwartz, who wasn't.

Karen closed her eyes as his hands moved onto her breast. She breathed his smell. Len's smell, and behind her eyes the face of John Sheridan came, went, mixed with Len's. It wasn't bad to think of John.

"What!" Schwartz jumped back.

God, had she said anything? Oh, God, had she said his name out loud?

It was all right. Thank God he was only shouting, *"Where* does she work at the Met?"

7

South of Naarden, twenty miles east of Amsterdam, the country road across the wide canal became spectacular. Behind it, mile after mile, ran exquisite old estates. There was a scaled-down castle on a tiny moat; another was a white rococo fantasy, all white and swirling and windowy behind its always open iron gates. But the Baron Wartena's estate was the most classically Dutch: three red-brick houses of the early eighteenth century; a main house set back a hundred yards from two flanking houses at right angles, forming a great grass courtyard, now thick with crocuses of white, purple and gold. All three houses were two-storied, the main house not that much larger than the guest-house and the servants' house, but higher, with its steep-pitched roof and white stone balustrade. And magnificent with a double stairway to the main door. Architects and amateurs agreed: the genius of the place, buildings, trees and setting, lay in its subtle asymmetry.

The Baron Wartena had heard this hundreds of times over the years. And each time he listened with the same deep smile, not only since it was polite but since he loved his house the way a father loves his lovely only child. Once, with friends, when the talk had gone that way at the end of a dinner memorable for its fine wine, and someone said jokingly, "Piet would kill for that house of his," Wartena had said, "I have."

Nothing more than that. And the table had gone quiet as each thought back to the war and the horrors of the Nazi occupation.

Now Wartena turned from his awful guest to consider this "proposal." True, it wasn't Den Roothuis, but the farm buildings at Ouderkerk were also like family. They were devils to want that.

The old man turned. "No. Not the old barn."

"It would be best, Baron Wartena."

"You will not!" The baron felt the rage rising from his stomach, shortening his breath. If he were thirty years younger, he would thrash . . . He steadied himself at the edge of the table. His hands had liver spots the color of the oak he gripped. He calmed himself enough to speak.

"We have discussed the matter. Kill him if you must, but leave my buildings be, sir!"

"Certainly, Baron," said the man, rising to leave.

The old man refused his hand. He smiled and walked away, taking a last admiring look at the sea battle raging over the empty fireplace.

~~~~~~ **8**

Karen was in London, thanks to her publishers. Schwartz went with her, grudging courtesy of the New York PD. He stayed one day; then they both agreed he'd better go on to Holland. He was impossible, in one of his crazy "Jake" moods. Schwartz was convinced that everything was spoiled forever between him and his son.

Karen knew it was a phase; Jake didn't want to know either of them just now. Nineteen and breaking away from home, that's all. So she'd shrug and pick up the telephone. Not Schwartz. Schwartz waited for the kid to call him. Sometimes, at the end of Karen's call, he'd slouch to the phone with a gruff "Hi, hotshot. How goes it?" and be heartsick when all he got was an "OK" in his ear from a great distance.

Karen was furious. Why were fathers such assholes with sons? But she couldn't say anything, of course.

Now, as the plane lands at Schiphol, Schwartz is remembering Jake as a kid of four or five, hugging and wrestling and the love they had. And then, because such is Schwartz, who thinks that maybe all men are like this but how the hell should he know, he finds the Jake pains leaving his mind. It's being on the job again, as he likes it, on his own.

Just about. There's a contact at the Dutch police. He checks in and finds nothing there. Interpol has nothing; why should the Dutch? He finds, as he already knows, that he can't carry a gun. Fine with him. If he needs protection, they'll assign someone. Perhaps he'd like a driver? No, thanks, he wouldn't. But he takes a contact name and number just in case. And no, he wouldn't mind calling in to tell them how it's going. And could they recommend a hotel? They call one for him. Good. Now they know where to reach him.

It's a nice, comfortable place across the park from the Rijks Museum in homely, comfortable turn-of-the-century Amsterdam. Not in the stunning and stunningly cramped old town. So he tells Karen on the phone, who knows from this he's better. He misses her. She's coming over in three days. He's glad.

Then he showers, stands naked wondering what to do, puts on his track suit, runs around the park for an hour, comes back to his room, showers again, dresses, goes down to the hotel restaurant for dinner and a lager. Then he's back up in his room in T-shirt and underpants, maps and his own diagrams spread over the chenille bedspread. He knows this bit his finger's on. He checks another map. It's only a short bus ride up the Amstel. Ouderkerk. Old church. That's about the extent of his Dutch, that and *gotverdommen*. Some combination. But everyone speaks English here. He'll get to Ouderkerk tomorrow.

And just as he's getting to sleep, Jake's face comes to him and his hand pats the blanket as if it were a small boy's hair.

9

A light rain was falling when Schwartz got off the bus. He turned up his raincoat collar, pulled his hat down and went for the closest café, at the next corner. Inside he had coffee and looked at the map and its blow-up diagram. A sort of suburb now, Ouderkerk, but the farmlands beginning behind it. So if he followed the main street upriver, took a right, it should be about half a mile to where those paintings were found. He looked across the carpet-covered tables through the window. Even sodden, it was a postcard town: old white clapboard, shutters, the roofs slanting higgledy-piggledy in shining tiles.

Walking through it, Schwartz saw the antique shops, the so-discreet signs of retail stores and decided, no, thanks, not for him, living in a public dollhouse. But it got better, as he moved away from the center. Ramshackle barns, comfortable-looking farmhouses, some windmills. And then the flat, flat fields. Black and light green. He looked at his diagram. It should be down there where the fields were great blocks of white, red, purple and gold. The tulips. And back in there. He squinted. There was the windmill and those buildings behind it.

Once in sight, the buildings seemed to get no closer. Holland was strange. Everything was jammed together, but you went off a road and it became an infinity of flatness with a windmill. Schwartz felt some unexplainable excitement. He left the hard road and followed the dirt one on the low dike separating the fields. Now he was closer. He made out the pasture that went to the buildings and in back of them the tulip fields, bright patchwork even in the rain. He thought of what he'd look for. He didn't know. Something that fit, something that didn't.

Now he was closer. He could see these were old farm buildings, older than he'd seen before. Out of an old Dutch painting. Cows, the windmill and huddle of buildings, shaggy thatched house, smoke curling up slowly from the barn, the stand of poplars.

Smoke curling up from the barn? Schwartz stopped. He looked. Yes, it was, and heavier. He started to run. Jesus, the barn was really on fire. He ran towards the windmill, shouting, "Fire! Fire!" and "Help!" and "Hey!" Nobody.

He ran past the windmill, shouting into the farmyard. Some cows mooed.

He ran to the barn door and tried to pull it open. It was stuck; he wasn't getting it the right way. He lifted hard and pulled, and it opened. Schwartz looked in and down the barn to where the fire was burning. It couldn't have been going long. He'd go to the house. . . . No animals inside, good. Then he saw the shadow between him and the fire. It moved a little. He didn't like guns, but now he wanted one.

Then Schwartz saw what made the shadow and he knew he didn't need a gun. Fifty feet in front of him, and twelve above, a man hung by his neck from a rope on a rafter. Schwartz walked up. The man was heavy, but so was the rope around his neck. His eyes bulged wide and his tongue stuck out. He was dead. Blue-purple and dead. Schwartz coughed with the smoke. There was the ladder up to the loft. He looked at the fire and back to the slowly swinging man. Yes, dead. The farmer? He'd better call. He turned back again. Not a farmer. Not those long, uncalloused hands in the firelight.

Schwartz ran out of the barn. "Hey, hey!" he called across the farmyard.

He banged on the door and went into the house. Nothing, nobody. He looked for the phone. No phone. Marvelous. Shit! He ran through the house looking for—for what? Corpses. Nobody. "Shit, shit, shit. OK, calm down, shithead," he said out loud. No phone. A hanged man in a burning barn miles from anything. And all this flat, flat . . . Wait, the windmill.

Schwartz ran out across the farmyard. The fire didn't seem worse. Where the hell was the door on this thing? There. He went in. Nobody, of course. No phone, of course. Worktables, white wood, bare. He went up the steps. Then it got darker and the steps became small and steep. Then there was no light at all, and he was climbing a ladder in that smell. What had they milled here—linseed? No more ladder. A sliver of light he went toward. Sat back on something and kicked and kicked it open and almost out as the flap opened right over the axle of the wind sail. Jesus. There was the town, not close enough, too far.

He hung out by one arm, looked the other way down over the tulip fields. Wait, someone was walking down there in a yellow rain suit. "Hey, hey!" Schwartz screamed. Not a thing. Had the person been here? At least he was the closest help; maybe he'd know the area, thought Schwartz. The smoke came up from the barn no faster and no slower than before.

Schwartz came down, jogged through the farmyard, stopped at the edge, wondering whether the fire would burn slower with the barn door open or closed, decided he hadn't a clue and ran off into the tulips after the walker.

Where had he gone? Schwartz looked in the direction he'd seen him. Disappeared? No, there he was, way off there. He'd been in the yellow field. Now his yellow showed against the dark red tulips. All right, and Schwartz ran off the path down into white tulips. The earth was too soft; it wasn't worth the straight line. He'd go back to the path and catch him.

Schwartz ran and ran. Now he could see the figure clearly, a tall yellow figure along the purple tulip horizon.

Schwartz ran. Linseed, that's not what windmills . . . That's from oil paint. He must be close enough now.

"Hey! Hey! Hi! Hey!"

No. The figure walked on.

Schwartz put in a sprint. He felt the mud come up under his trouser cuffs. OK, now.

"Hey! Hey!"

The figure turned.

Schwartz slowed down; it was OK now.

The figure in yellow turned away and started running.

~~~~~~~~ **10**

Schwartz was gaining on the running figure. He still wasn't close enough to see him distinctly, but he could see he was very tall, dressed in a yellow hooded suit, the kind worn for running in the rain. His own raincoat and tweed sports jacket and woolen trousers were not what you wore running in the rain. You were very sticky in them. And constricted and uncomfortable. The trousers were pulling up into Schwartz's groin. But on this dirt road—so long and straight it went into a near horizon—he'd catch the man in yellow.

Red, pink and white fields of tulips. Schwartz got closer. Dressed right or not, it didn't matter. If that was who murdered that man and set the fire, he'd had a full morning before the run. He'd be tiring now. Thinking this gave Schwartz more energy. Got into a rhythm. Pink, red and dark purple tulips. Millions. Murdered? Well, it had to be. Or why running away?

The road in front of Schwartz was empty. Schwartz stopped, looked and smiled. "Oh, no, wise guy, I saw that one at the windmill," he said in long, hard breaths, looking at the field of yellow tulips two hundred yards or so in front, to his left. He ran down the path and turned into the field. Something was there at the other end, a small barn.

He'd be there. What if he had a gun? The question seemed silly to Schwartz since he'd asked it too late. He thought, It's what I'm paid for, crashed through the final patch of tulips and almost fell into the water. And it wasn't a barn either.

It was a small boathouse. Schwartz ran into it and out onto its dock just in time to see the man in yellow rounding a bend out of sight in a heavy rowing boat.

He looked around. Nobody. Of course. Another boat in the boathouse, a racing scull. He lifted it off the rack and carried it awkwardly to the water and put it in. Then Schwartz remembered oars and took the boat out of the water and turned it onto the dock and went back in and found two oars and went back out and set them on the dock and put the scull back into the water and pulled his trousers out of his groin and held the boat's metal outrigger and took one oar and leaned out to the outrigger over the water. And then it started coming to him that he was in some sort of trouble here. But he kept fiddling around, figuring how to get the oars in. He knew rowboats, of course—Central Park, Prospect Park, once even in Regent's Park in London. Nice, fat, heavy idiot-simple rowboats. But this! Jesus. At Harvard once a friend of his got him into one on the dock of Weld Boathouse. He'd been in it about two minutes before giving up, terrified of capsizing or of breaking the thing. He kept fiddling. There. Now you were supposed to step onto that strut stuff, not into the boat's thin skin. He remembered, your foot would go right through. He told himself to hurry up, and then he told himself to shut up and slow down.

OK. So he was standing with one foot on the dock, and no, the clothes were all wrong. Schwartz took off his hat, raincoat, sports jacket and shoes, wrapped them into a bundle and put them . . . There was no damned place. So he put his shoes in and left the rest on the dock. He got in. The boat seemed to tip over but didn't. He tried to keep it balanced on the oar flat out on the water. That was it. It wasn't so hard. He sat down on the wooden seat. It slipped back on its track. The boat wanted to turn over. Then he had his feet into those leather things. He'd seen them do that. Now. It wasn't so hard. He slowly pushed the boat off with his hand, then with the edge of the dockside oar. It wasn't so hard. Now he was on the water. It was so hard.

He slid forward slowly, looking at the oars dragging back flat. All right, so now you turned your wrists and dug in and . . .

The boat shook. One oar pulled down deeper and deeper into the water so that Schwartz couldn't seem to let go. The boat spun; water lapped in over his woolen trousers. Calm down. Don't panic. The wrists. Yes. He felt the oar slip out. OK, so not so deep and you kept pulling both oars evenly and you used your legs to push back. He did it. The boat was moving! Then his hands were at his stomach and the water kept pushing them with the oar handles into his stomach. Oh, you had to turn your wrists there, too, to get the oars out. Then you slid forward, slowly, and you turned your wrists to put the oar blades in and then you pulled back and pushed back with your legs. And hey. He was doing it. The goddamned thing was moving.

Backwards! That's right, these things went backwards. Shit. Schwartz turned the scull around with one oar. OK, steering was like any rowboat. This was better. Now he was going with the current. It was probably some river. He didn't want to think about the man he was following just yet. He thought the man he was following was probably passing New Orleans by then.

Schwartz began rowing in a tentative, wobbly way, but rowing, looking back at every stroke to see where he was headed. He took gentle strokes and felt better. Here came a bridge. Plenty of room.

An oar hit the stone pier. Shit, shit! He pushed off. The boat kept moving in the current. But stroke after stroke, Schwartz felt better, less panicky.

Tuilps had ended. Nothing but flat fields of grass down to the sloped stone-block banks. Turn after turn. He hit two more bridges but went through three others without hitting. Then he started to recognize the buildings of Ouderkerk. Then he saw that this river was going to join another. He knew that it was the Amstel and that he'd have to go with the current. If the man in yellow had gone the other way—well, that was that.

There were some boys watching from the bridge where the rivers joined.

"Hey!" Schwartz yelled.

"Hey!" they called back, smiling.

Schwartz was afraid to let go of the oar. He tried to indicate himself by nodding down. "Police, police." He nodded down. Then he yelled, "Fire! Fire!," indicating its direction by twisting his head back.

The boys smiled down at the man rowing a skiff in shirt and tie and trousers, jerking his head about and shouting in English. One leaned over. "Hey, man, you English?"

"Yes. English. No, American. Police. There's a fire there. Call the police, the fire department, I mean," Schwartz was yelling, by this time under the bridge. He came out the other side.

One of the boys had crossed. "Hey, man," he shouted down, "hey, Mr. No American Police Fireman. You're crazy, man. You're too much! Bye!"

"No," Schwartz tried to shout, but he had to concentrate on turning into the stronger current.

Now he was on the Amstel, passing Ouderkerk, dabbing at the water, grabbing lightly at it in the strong current. He was surprised at how fast he was moving.

The rain was coming down harder. Should he pull in? But if . . . He let the oars rest on the water and turned his head around. Behind him, in front of the boat, the river widened. And there . . . Jesus! There he was. It had to be, maybe half a mile down. The yellow, the heavy boat. No, he'd follow him. No reason he'd be recognized without his hat or raincoat. Besides, who'd think he'd have followed in a single scull? So the guy wouldn't be exactly racing. The element of surprise? And this boat moved faster in the current, didn't it? Sure it did. Schwartz began rowing again, trying to keep the scull in something of a straight line.

A barge was coming downstream. No problem. He'd just move to the side a bit. Holy shit, the barge was almost on him!

Twenty feet on his left, the barge chugged past, pushing up big swells of water. Schwartz put the oar blades flat out to steady the boat. Here they came. He shut his eyes. He was going to sink right there. He felt the water, the rise up and down, the side-to-side rocking. Heard some slop in. Less rocking. He opened his eyes. Still afloat. A few inches of water sloshed up and down the bottom of the scull. All right, he said to himself, that wasn't so bad, Inspector. And it wasn't.

What were so bad, as he started pulling on the oars again, were the blisters on his thumbs and at the bases of his middle fingers. And what was worse than so bad was the searing, stiff pain in his wrists.

But Schwartz kept going. And when he turned, he saw that he was, he seemed to be, getting closer.

Now Schwartz was coming into Amsterdam. More boats on the river, more wake, wash, waves. He'd ride it out. He'd stay on the other side from the man in yellow, unnoticed. It could work. He'd gone through the pain. He could imagine its coming again, but he could imagine going through it again. A racing eight passed him as if he were anchored. Now there were a lot of rowing boats and the river was wide. He couldn't get their help. Maybe they'd take him seriously, but it would tip off the man in yellow, who could pull in anywhere and disappear. Where the hell was he heading anyway?

Schwartz glanced at his watch as he slid forward. Jesus, maybe two hours of this already. He went under a bridge and looked back. A quarter of a mile ahead of him, the man in yellow was turning off into a side canal. It looked as if he were pausing, looking upriver. Schwartz came out from under the bridge trying to look like a casual sculler. Ho-ho. He turned again. Yes, the boat was going into that canal.

Maybe it was the pain coming around again, but as he started his ridiculous turn downstream, under the bridge into the canal, Schwartz felt that he'd so far been very lucky with this matchstick of a boat. And he felt that now his luck was running out. For one thing, he'd run out of current to move him along. And what if he met a big barge on this narrow canal?

But Schwartz kept rowing. Something inside him told him to keep rowing. He looked back. Now the man in yellow had to know. He was staying that quarter mile ahead.

Sixty degrees and a steady, cold rain now, Schwartz was thinking, but he'd stay warm enough as long as he kept rowing. There was room for another boat to pass, too. Just. But Schwartz didn't see it coming out of a side canal. Schwartz was in the middle. He heard the outboard motor, then felt the oar blade hit. The scull spun. Water poured in. The man steering the outboard was swearing in Dutch. He looked at Schwartz and started laughing. Schwartz looked at the half oar blade and started swearing. The man in yellow turned off into another canal; Schwartz saw that.

When he came down to the turn, he began to realize what a narrow canal might be like. He understood that he had been on a wide one. Here there was room for just one boat. The oars didn't help. The occasional moored barges didn't help. Nor did the garbage and wood floating, banging into him, ruining whatever tentative rhythm he'd managed to get up, what with the blisters, the wrists, the wet wool rubbing his groin raw and the broken oar. And the wet wool rubbing, burning into the left side of his groin. If he dared let go of the oars, if he dared stand in the boat, he would have taken his pants off. After all, how much stupider could he have looked? But he didn't dare.

He put his head back and opened his mouth to the rain. There. That felt better. He'd show that fucker in yellow.

Banging into boats and logs and bridges, turning and missing turns and somehow backing up and turning and half using his oars sometimes as poles, Schwartz followed the other boat. Canal after canal. The kind of tour you have to pay for, he thought as he turned into a canal and looked back to see under bridge after bridge after bridge, six or seven in a row, down to, way down to the steady rowing of the man in yellow. What a pretty picture, Schwartz thought. Schwartz thought many things, including: Wasn't there a better way of catching up? But he figured there wasn't.

He looked up occasionally at people on the streets,

bridges, at people whistling or laughing or calling out to him. Once he yelled, "Fire at Ouderkerk, a fire south of Ouderkerk," up to a man, who nodded and said, calmly, that he'd telephone. That had been back in the old section, and it had struck Schwartz, that man's calm answer, that up there was an ordinary sane world, and what the fuck was he doing down here? What? That was an hour ago.

Now it was some sort of industrial section, factory walls, warehouses; he could have followed only by canal. And the canals were beginning to widen. Some luck, again. No big boats here. Just as well. They'd crush this like the matchstick it was.

And the man in yellow with the slower boat, just hanging that same distance ahead. There he was, down there where the canal seemed to be coming into . . .

It was when Schwartz saw the dock cranes, only then that something began bothering him. He kept rowing. Why hadn't that man lost him in the canal system? Christ, it wouldn't have been too hard. Maybe he didn't know it too well himself? Maybe he had to get to wherever the hell he was heading? Or maybe . . . Schwartz kept rowing. If he stopped, the weight of the idea coming to him would sink the boat with him strapped in it like a millstone. He looked around again. There he was, slowly, effortlessly rowing. Of course, he could have lost him. That guy didn't want to, could row rings around him, heavy boat or not.

Schwartz kept rowing. Screw it, he thought. In for a penny . . . in for a pounding.

Here the canal walls were steep. Steel ladders went up. He could stop. He shut his eyes. No. He opened them. The gray light was sinking. The rain was heavy now. Schwartz kept rowing, rowing, rowing.

"Whoooo."

He nearly jumped out of the boat. A horn. What? He turned around as the scull came out of the canal.

Oh, shit. No. Oh, come on, gimme a break! he said to himself, the little boat, the rain, to the man in yellow no more than three hundred yards away. To the tankers and freighters moving before him in the harbor of Amsterdam.

~~~~~~~ 11

There were waves out there, real waves. And wind and rain and darkness and big ships. And Schwartz couldn't really row. Every reason to stop. And now, a few hundred yards out, bobbing up and down, the man in yellow rested easily on his oars, watching, waiting for him to turn back.

And probably smiling, thought Schwartz, starting to turn back into the canal.

And probably still smiling, thought Schwartz, turning past the canal, turning until the scull pointed out again and rowing into the harbor, whose other side he only guessed by far-off lights.

Three strokes out Schwartz felt the wind blow hard. Ten strokes out the waves broke over the oilskin stern, and his oars went from being buried deep to breaking mid-stroke through the water into air; he fell back in the momentum, the oar blades locked underwater, the oars inboard crushed down on his upper chest. He let the handles go; the boat lurched and water poured over him. But the oars lifted away.

Schwartz pulled himself up and found the handles. The scull was half full of water, salt water, he noticed, licking his lips. OK. So far, so good. He couldn't believe this was happening. Still, the little matchstick was afloat. He looked to see the other boat moving steadily away across the harbor. Its heaviness was now, Schwartz saw, to its advantage. Well, he thought, he needs something to even the odds. At least he hasn't got a gun or cannon mounted back there.

Schwartz rowed again but now with shorter strokes to keep his balance. The wind blew him farther into the harbor. He thought maybe the wind would do it. Maybe if he kept the blade up and down like little sails to catch the wind . . . He stopped. A wall of steel was just about to crush him. He dropped his oars into the water and pulled on one to turn, the other to stop the boat. He shouted, "Hey! Hey! Watch it!" He kept turning the scull in a circle, shouting, "Watch it!" and "Hey!" Then he started laughing at the craziness of shouting at the moving wall. Then he stopped laughing and tried to cope with its wake.

It passed. Miraculous. And somehow this little scull full of water was still afloat. It was a detail, but it made Schwartz smile. Then it made his heart race. The freighter had passed about fifteen feet from him. He figured shouting at it had been like shouting at an apartment block. Worse—the freighter had no windows. Only someone up there on its roof happening to lean over to look at the street way down below could have seen him. And who'd be leaning from the roof in this weather? Oh, Jesus, Schwartz thought, and even if they saw me, what could they do? That scared him into rowing again.

Now he saw moving lights, heard over and beneath the wind and rain and wave-slap the turn of heavy engines and the ships' hoot-hoots.

No point in trying to row back, not with the boat full of water and the wind. No point, really, in rowing at all. Anywhere he was going to get, he'd get by wind and current. If at all. If at all. OK. The best he could do was sit and steer. At least now he could turn the scull and face wherever he was going.

So he turned the boat around and saw the rough wooden handles stained red-pink either side of his hands and knew it was his own blood and didn't bother lifting his hands to look. Schwartz sat there feeling very silly and very sad.

Then he looked up and didn't feel sad. He was closer to the other boat than he'd been all day. All day, he repeated to himself. The yellow rain hood kept him from seeing the man's features, but this was better, being able to look straight at him. Much better, catching up with him, even though he was rowing steadily, powerfully. He'd catch up at this rate.

He had to see Schwartz getting closer. Doing nothing but getting closer. He'd bet the man in yellow wasn't smiling now.

They were somewhere in the middle of the darkened harbor. Lights were swinging past them, crossing the waves between them, behind them and in front. A noise of ships' horns. Bells. The other man stopped rowing. Something was coming up behind Schwartz, off to his left. But he kept watching the man in yellow. Maybe the light would hit him. Maybe the hood would blow off.

Thirty yards away, it wasn't more, and Schwartz didn't even see it, didn't even hear it. Just felt it, a tremendous sudden bee sting, a thick needle in the middle of his right shoulder. "Oh, fucking terrific!" he shouted. "Guns, bullets. Fucking wonderful! That's all that was missing here!" The blood poured down his shirt sleeve. He watched his right hand go limp, open, the oar handle bob away from his hand.

Schwartz thought, When the blood reaches the back of my hand, I'm going to stand up in this fucking matchstick and warn that bastard I've got a secret weapon—my Jewish sense of humor! He knew this was silly. He was very scared, a moving, sitting target. He started sliding down into the boat.

Then a light swung across his eyes, and he heard a voice and then no voice but water and a crash and the boat turning over on him and hitting his head and coming up but not up, still underwater and managing to pull his feet out and then coming up and a tremendous crack on his head and seeing Jake and Karen as he sank, his beautiful little Jake.

~~~~~~~~ **12**

One Amsterdam newspaper gave a few lines on an inside page to a boating accident in the harbor. Another, *Den Telegraaf*, gave several paragraphs to the apparent suicide in an Ouderkerk barn of a Rudolph Ten Eyck, sixty-nine years old, estate manager for Baron Piet Wartena.

Two days later the larger story broke. Exclusive to *Den Telegraaf*, copies of documents had been received linking Ten Eyck to Nazi war crimes in Holland in 1943. A very poor photograph showed a young smiling man named as Ten Eyck in the uniform of the Waffen SS. The documents clearly indicated Ten Eyck to have been "Butcher Rudi," whose zeal for the Third Reich in rounding up resistance, Jews, socialists, et cetera, for deportation was such that many of them had died before reaching the trains. The police and War Crimes Authority were investigating.

The next day the story had been picked up by the international press. The *Times* of London ended its coverage suggesting the suicide might have been linked to the exposure of Ten Eyck as a war criminal. The *Christian Science Monitor* ran a small, hopeful editorial on the human conscience. And a blurb in the *New York Post* ran under the title DUTCHMAN SWINGS—RED SPY LINK?

In the middle of this Schwartz woke up to bright sunshine. He shut his eyes again. Then he opened them and said, "Oh." Karen sat by the bed, holding his hand.

"Sweetheart." She leaned over him. "You were calling my name and Jake's."

"Oh."

"Jake's been calling every few hours. He wants to speak to you when you can."

"Oh."

"Are you in much pain, darling?"

Schwartz looked at Karen. "No," he said, and shook his head, bringing great stabs of pain through his shoulder blade. "Yes, a bit."

He lifted Karen's hand, and she brought it to his mouth for him to kiss. Then she pulled his lip. He smiled.

"You were lucky."

"What, that they didn't use depth charges?"

"To be fished out like that."

"Don't tell me. It was Gallagher who just happened to be water-skiing from a helicopter. . . ."

"The boat that hit you was a harbor launch. A bigger ship wouldn't have noticed."

"Yeah? Tell me more good news," Schwartz said, beginning to look around.

"Your shoulder. The bullet was deep but hasn't permanently damaged any tendon or bone."

"Good. And the other guy?"

"No other guy, Len. Amsterdam or New York, I'm just a cop's wife to you people. They haven't told me anything. But there must be something. One of them's sitting outside the door. Wants to talk to you when you're ready. Actually they've been very nice to me. Len, is he guarding you from something?"

Schwartz looked at Karen. His eye caught an enormous bouquet of tulips—white tulips, pink tulips, red tulips, purple tulips. He thought he might be sick. Instead, he smiled. "Thanks for the flowers."

"Len."

"No, I mean, I wish he were guarding me. It would mean someone's finally taking this seriously. Honey, look, all they know is someone's shot a high-ranking American cop visiting their fair city. Of course, they'll post someone out there. But no one's coming after me." He almost added, "Not here, anyway," but thought better of it.

"OK. I'm sorry, Len. I hate this. All these years and you . . . I hate this, you here with a bullet in your shoulder—" Karen stopped, her eyes darkened with tears.

"Hey, the bullet's out, right? And you're right, I have been lucky, and now, statistically, I'm even safer, right? I've had the bullet most cops don't get."

179

"Times like this . . . Well," she said, anger in her voice, "you really are a cop, aren't you?"

Schwartz smiled. "Guilty as charged."

"I mean," Karen said, angry and starting to laugh, "seventeen years, and I still don't know how I feel about it. Damn it and you!" and she stood up and bent over and kissed him and told him she adored him.

Later he talked with the Dutch detective, whose name he first heard as Go Wink and Nod but later saw was Bo Winkenoog. It was a tossup as to who was interviewing whom.

No, they hadn't seen this man in yellow. No, he didn't know who it could be who'd shot him. They'd found the boat across the harbor where it belonged. Owned by a brickyard, hadn't been missed. No, the barn had pretty well stopped burning in the rain. No, Schwartz hadn't known the hanged man. No, the autopsy showed nothing inconsistent with suicide. No, Schwartz had no special reason for thinking anything else, except the man in yellow and all this bandaging on his right shoulder. Yes, indeed, he seems to have been this pig of a Nazi, the worst kind to the Dutch, a Dutch Nazi. His prints on the documents. And yes, they, too, knew the place was where those paintings had been found. Nothing to show he was anything but the farm manager for Wartena. But yes, of course, they'd put together some biographical data on this Ten Eyck and on Wartena and the discovery of the paintings. And they hoped their distinguished American colleague would not think badly of them or of Amsterdam because of . . . No, no, of course not. He loved it. Everything. Canals, tulips.

And then, with the pain and the drugs and the start of a horrific physiotherapy and a series of stammering, enraging, wonderful phone calls with Jake, these talks went on for two days.

Schwartz told them as little as possible, consistent with professional good manners. Ditto from them. Nothing much or nothing more than circumstantial. Still, it all fit.

And no, Winkenoog replied, polite, puzzled. He did not see anything more than strange coincidence in all this happening when the inspector chose to visit. Did the inspector think . . . ?

No, not really. The inspector really didn't think.

~~~~~ 13

The inspector thought, Schwartz thought, it wasn't coincidence. He'd been lucky or they'd been unlucky—or was it vice versa—but anyway, they knew he was on to them. And they knew, somehow, through this man or woman at the Met.

Between groans and fidgets Schwartz said as much to Karen on the flight back to New York, but he wouldn't go back on to painkillers. He didn't think it was Karen's acquaintance Georgia. Karen should go on as before and not let on. No, he'd make it without a painkiller. But, and this was serious, now Karen must let him know, really report everything she said, did, heard concerning the case. Schwartz was in the toilet when the plane hit the big air pocket. He came back to the seat gray-faced and took a painkiller.

In New York everyone was concerned, for reasons

so different it amused him. Jake's was best. Real concern, curiosity, even some bits of pride leaked through Yale's freshman starting second baseman. Bob's was next best, the kind he wished Jake had, well, could show like that. That first morning Bob hung around and hung around, finally asking if Schwartz had received his telegram. Schwartz spent the rest of the day thanking Bob and wondering if he had received it. He wondered if Bob had addressed it to him as "sir."

Gallagher's concern, of course, was trickier: tremendously warm and personal over the phone, the call ending with a request as good as a summons for a full status case review.

It was at the end of that meeting, in his office piled with documents, notes, photocopies, maps, charts, slide projector, screen, even a sample x-ray of an old painting, that Schwartz laughed and said it seemed more a dissertation for a Ph.D. in fine arts than a case. And he knew before he finished saying it that he'd put his foot in his mouth up to about his knee.

And sure enough, Gallagher picked him up on it, said, "Exactly the trouble, Lenny," and six grown men looked away from Schwartz as one averts one's face from catastrophe.

And then Gallagher astounded everyone by saying, "Nevertheless, Lenny's theory is the best one going. And I personally am convinced by what happened over there in Holland. So this team should know it has the full support of everyone, and I mean everyone right up to the . . . well, everyone."

Schwartz decided he couldn't take this support from Gallagher lying down, so he added that yes, that was all very well, but all they still had was worth diddly-squat in court on a murder charge or accessory charge or conspiracy charge. Then the others joined in saying, yeah, you couldn't pull in museum bigwigs as if they were alphabet city dope peddlers. That what they wanted to know was what the hell they were supposed to do now?

Then Gallagher and Schwartz looked at each other, and Schwartz asked everyone else to leave the room. Then Gallagher said, yes, he, too, was sort of wondering what Schwartz had in mind.

Schwartz rotated his shoulder and winced. "Maybe it's time," he said, "to lie."

BOOK IV

———— **1**

"**C**humminess," he'd admit, was a possible style. He knew three or four curators and department chairmen, good at their jobs, who were like that. But "chumminess" was not for Gerald Vandevelde.

Not that his style was unfriendly; that, after all, wasn't the opposite of informality. It was formal, mannered, or, if you would, courtly, or, if you would, elegant. It was very fair. It treated the newest parttime assistant exactly as it did his curator or administrator. It was successful because in the distance it set between himself and others what each was doing could be seen and understood and, so, assessed. It depended, naturally, on real ability; the manners couldn't be a mask for emptiness.

He had maintained, developed and built this great department through his talents and hard work. A tremendous energy, a way of bringing in gifts, bequests, donations, trust funds the envy of other European painting departments around the world. A reputation in the field based on a bookshelf, now, of writing—not popular but scholarly and not without an elegance of style.

And the eye, the famous Vandevelde eye, which had time after time made the right choices, said, "Not really," to the possibilities that weren't quite on, infallibly said yes to those that were and, best of all, been proven correct in the unsuspected, half-undiscovered world of "maybe" masterworks picked up for the museum at a tenth their true market values: the Velázquez *Soldier of Philip IV* and the Fabritius *Rachel at the Well* being merely the two for which he felt most pride in the past few years.

The department ran, then, by his example. And the department ran well. Problems, of course. But always the perspective to see them and, seeing them, to solve them.

But this was a new and bothersome one, this one of Georgia and Johnnie Sheridan. Yes, staff had private lives and others had their work affected; besotment had been seen before. But hardly so high up in the department. And they'd hardly run such risks, one sign of this besotment being that Georgia must be assuming that he, Vandevelde, hadn't a clue. And another thing . . .

And *the* other thing: Where was old Johnnie in all this? The recluse suddenly much "in" things. And so close? And then, when one tried to find out, tried so professionally, there was the recluse again, so that one didn't know *whom* one was dealing with.

Or perhaps not dealing with, but no, on the whole, he was going for "dealing with," though it seemed just too preposterous.

Nevertheless, as with the paintings, one had to trust the eye, the feel of the situation, especially when the hard data were so very inconclusive. The question was, Who was chasing whom? A question. Another was, When would the police be around? Never? Highly improbable.

At any rate, with someone as formidable as Johnnie, the thing was to act—creatively, preemptively and soon.

2

You're getting smarter, she told herself. No, you're just getting older. She turned her cheek into the mirror and stared. No, you're getting smarter, too.

Georgia Morris felt she'd won the debate she'd been having with herself ever since Johnnie left town for a few weeks. That she'd "won" this morning after seeing him on his return last night seemed to cinch the victory. Over romance? No, not romance; over her self-destructive self.

He didn't love her. Probably couldn't love anyone. So he wasn't going to change. Would never love her. Her love for him wasn't going to make him love her. There. She could say it. So she didn't love him in that head-over-heels, sacrifice-anything-for-you-my-strong-man way anymore. God, it felt good, good, good to have that much control. To like yourself enough.

She brushed her hair.

Of course, she adored him, but that was different. That was his beautiful body. Sex, the sheer physical thrill of him. Yes, and a good escort. Intelligent, manners, all that. But not to slobber after, not to . . . not to live the way her mother had for thirty-five years with her father. Another heartless ego. Another mean prick.

Georgia's mouth pulled into a thin line. She shook her head a little, surprised and ashamed at the hardness of her language and the truth of what she'd thought.

Her mouth relaxed again. No, it was all right. And all right to know herself. All right to take those pleasures. And if he thrilled her, well, she thrilled him, too. Did he think she was *his* slave when she'd pulled him into that display bedroom up in Bloomingdale's and down behind that silly four-poster bed with his head between her legs, licking her even as they heard the people walking just out there in front, saying, "Ooh, c'mon. You've just gotta see this terrific colonial room."

So, yes, she'd taken what she wanted. But who would have guessed what she'd want? She laughed out loud. Like a month ago, when she'd first guessed what he was leading up to, hinting at, and she'd been so shocked. Her workplace? The sacrosanct MMA? But then the idea grew on her, though she'd still projected it all on to him. First in her office, though that was just her little office. Nice painting on the wall, but it could have been any of ten thousand after-hour offices across the city.

Then, a little more exciting, up in Photography over the great hall, up against the smooth, cool dome, her dress hitched up, the two of them like a sailor and whore in a doorway and hearing the guard's footsteps getting closer and rushing to finish and come before the guard appeared and straightening her clothes and walking past the guard saying, "Good night, Carlos," and Carlos with the little half bow saying, "Good night, Mees Morris, good night, sir." And feeling Johnnie's excitement. Well, and why not go on, even further than he'd hoped? Yes, it was different now. She'd call him. She'd say she had a treat for him tonight. A surprise. As a matter of fact, she had two. She'd meet him at the main desk at closing. That's all she'd let him know.

~~~~~~~~~ **3**

Sheridan had been surprised at the museum's security. It was both more intensive and more lax than he'd imagined. The great pieces were protected by light, laser, steel, glass, locks, wired rooms, TV monitors and, most and best, an enormous security staff, hundreds day and night.

On the other hand, especially with senior staff like Georgia, bringing him in after hours was a simple matter of signing in. And moving out of her office after hours into the collections was again just a matter of signing. And many of the smaller pieces, of lesser value only in a place like this, were in quite ordinary cases. He'd seen them unlocked with a key, curator and assistant fiddling around to place a small Etruscan statue or apostle spoon the way an assistant would a necktie in a shopwindow—except that here the assistant handled the "merchandise" with gloves.

Other things weren't so clear—like furniture. He'd been wondering about furniture, say, in the Lehman Collection. If you ran your hand over a boule desk, would it set off an alarm? Would someone see it on a TV screen? Or if you sat down on an old oak chair in the Untermeyer Collection?

Georgia's answers varied from saying that nothing would happen to saying there were photoelectric eyes everywhere to saying if he took a step closer to it, an alarm would go off. Or she'd say, as they walked, "I don't know. Let's see." And she'd touch a marquetry cabinet and nothing would happen. And then she'd smile and say it was an educated guess, but she wouldn't try it with anything in that group there, behind the waist-high barrier.

And he'd let it go at that. He wouldn't push. He'd find the right time. It was always a matter of timing.

Hers was perfect; she came down the main staircase as he was entering, telling the guard of his appointment.

They kissed hello, she checked him in at the main desk and they went up to her office. Sheridan asked if she'd hint at the surprise. She wouldn't. But she said there were two.

She sat him in her small, neatly cluttered office and excused herself. He watched her walk out in her white double-breasted jacket and skirt. She looked very smart, he thought. Very attractive.

Georgia came back with cold champagne and glasses. "Would you?" she asked, giving Sheridan the bottle.

"Happily. Now this is a surprise, but is it *the* surprise?"

"Just the prelude," she said, sitting on the corner of her desk in front of him.

Georgia lifted her glass and leant forward towards Sheridan. "To you, my darling, and to . . . surprise."

Sheridan nodded. "To surprise."

They drank in silence, looking at each other.

"You're . . ."

"You're . . ." both said at once.

"Georgia, you're very beautiful. You look . . . very powerful—a warrior queen."

"Thank you. Yes. I feel like that. I feel good-looking. I was about to say the same of you. You're the handsomest man I could imagine, Johnnie. You're great fun. And great pleasure. I want us always to be friends."

"Friends?"

"Yes. Lovers, too. But not at the expense of friendship. You know we don't talk about the future. While you've been away, I've been thinking that it's only fair we understand each other. I'm not interested in marriage. If I were, I'd want you, darling. But I'm not."

"Is this the surprise?" Sheridan asked with a wry smile.

"Of course not; I wouldn't have thought my feelings on this a surprise to you."

"No. No, not really. We have similar views then." He put a finger on her shin and ran it up and down.

"Good, darling," Georgia said, sliding off the desk and bending over him, her red hair brushing his face. "I wanted us to understand that so you'd know my surprises were surprises, not tricks." She kissed his ear and whispered, "Now, come with me."

They left the office, went back down the main staircase and turned into the long hall going west. As they

195

came into the medieval court, Georgia said that the surprise was the result of some research she'd done. "Both surprises," she added.

She signed in with security at the doors to the Engelhard Courtyard and walked across in its dim night light, the last red-blues of sunset filtering in on the trees and fountains, on the darkening stained glass. She took them through the opposite glass door into the American wing. They went down the corridor and turned left.

"You've always liked this, haven't you?" Georgia asked, stopping in front of a mahogany scroll sofa upholstered a flamboyant golden yellow.

"Yes. . . ."

"Sit on it. Go ahead, sit on it."

He did, smiling. "Will you join me?"

"Yes, darling," Georgia said, "like this," kneeling in front of him and unzipping his pants.

He shifted. She sucked his prick into her mouth. His hands moved through her hair; his thumbs circled the inner rims of her ears. His prick swelled in her mouth, swelled and went down into her throat, which pulsed wide and pulled tight, pulsed wide, pulled tight.

Sheridan's eyes were open, his head was back. He saw the camera overhead, set so it didn't cover the sofa.

His hands went to the back of her head. He pulled. Georgia pushed back. He let her move his hands off. She drew off his prick and licked it and stood up.

"We'll continue elsewhere," she said. "You have just enough time to—address yourself."

It was true. Sheridan fixed his pants, and they began

walking down the corridor when a security guard came in from the other end. Georgia showed her pass.

"Beauty, you've done your research well. Even the timing."

"Yes, but the timing's approximate, so there's that element of chance. There's a real risk we'll be caught by security."

"Fifty-fifty, would you say?"

"Yes, like that."

"Good."

She squeezed his arm. "I knew you'd like that, darling. Now let's tour Americana."

And in a room in old Virginia he kissed her breasts and ran his tongue over her nipples. They kissed in a Philadelphian drawing room on a sofa probably by Duncan Phyfe.

A guard saw them chatting near a Shaker bedstead; seconds earlier they'd been on it, Sheridan's hand at the top of Georgia's soft-skinned thigh.

On they went. In a Greek Revival parlor Sheridan sat on a straight-backed chair and Georgia sat on Sheridan, his fingers moistened, moving up her vulva, pulling back above her clitoris and rubbing it lightly.

But for his peripheral vision, they would have been caught on an 1810 settee in Baltimore, his heavy balls in Georgia's hands.

Ten o'clock, an hour before they'd have to leave. He licked her ass behind the neoclassical façade of the old Federal Reserve. Then she took him back out into the courtyard and down to the Frank Lloyd Wright Room.

She whispered, "Here. Here's where we end, you lovely fucker," and climbed over the barrier railing.

First, they walked around the room, touching the chairs, the lamps, the tables, touching each other all over the room. They went to the sofa at the far end and undressed, hanging their clothes over the books and magazines on the sofa's footwide wooden wings, except for his jacket, which he spread under them, its white silk lining up.

"Lie down," she said.

Sheridan lay down, his knees bending to fit the sofa. Georgia mounted him, her knees straddling his hips. She stretched up and felt his stiff prick touching her labia, pushing them apart, sliding down her vulva, then up into her.

He felt her deeper, deeper, closing on him. Her hair as she leaned forward brushed his neck, his throat, hung over his face. He held her hips. He arched up, sliding in. Then back. Slowly up in all the way and back. She was red velvet.

She sat so that his prick pulled back onto her vulva, pushing back her clitoris. She pulled her hips back so she could feel him there. There and the fullness in her coming back down. Back and back down. And slowly faster, her face down into the side of his neck, the sweat smell of him.

He slid his hands back up from her hips onto her ass, the flesh globed smooth under his curving hands. Faster back and forth and slowly faster. His hand moving down the cleft, feeling the sweat on his belly hair, feeling the flesh of her belly, feeling her inside so he felt palm trees the flamethrower fuck the gooks like he couldn't tell if it was him in her or her in him how could you tell who was who so fuck them men kill them all.

"Oh, God, Johnnie." She came forward feeling herself opening everywhere opening and opening his fingers feeling them fill her push my God oh against his prick and here the waves, the waves.

They arched, they curved faster. She came, swallowing her groans, groaning through the long, high waves through her mouth, which opened onto him. And he was coming, hot in her, hot, the flamethrower, he groaned into her mouth.

They hung together hot, wet, the craziness turned to a tingling. Then the tingling to a chill and she said they'd better hurry and they did, but only by cheating, her underwear and his in both pockets of his sports jacket as they walked out of the well-crafted room past the security woman, who walked in.

In the cab to her apartment she asked if he was ready for the second surprise. He nodded.

"This time," Georgia said, "You do get hints. It's something I found. I'll show you at home. It's about Karen Walker. You know. Remember? That Horvay business? And something I've found. And my boss. Your friend Bobo Vandevelde."

"Oh?" said Sheridan, trying to sound not too interested.

Sheridan made omelets and salad and smiled to see Georgia's appetite. He could have casually brought it up but waited. She would.

She took more salad. "That other surprise. You know how I've been keeping my eyes open for Karen Walker, the art historian, the one whose husband—oh, of course you know. Well, it's become something of a problem."

"What's that?"

"A moral problem. What would you do if you found something that might implicate your boss? Your boss, whom you respected and admired?"

"That depends on what it was and how sure you were. You've found something?"

"I think so. We keep files on dealers and collectors, and while looking through them to see if we had something Karen didn't have, I found the material on Horvay's discoveries was substantially missing. And then last week I found it all in Vandevelde's office, in his own research files."

"But there's nothing strange in that. He might well have been curious to see them again, what with Horvay's murder, and the police coming around and—"

"They haven't, actually. I mean, only right after. Not even a detective, I remember. And no one since."

"I see. Still, it doesn't seem—"

"No. It's the notes with them."

"What about them?"

"I'll show you. I made photocopies. Wait."

Sheridan took a green apple from the fruit basket, put it on the side plate and began cutting it, carefully.

"Here, darling, look at this," she said at his side, putting the papers in front of him.

Her hair brushed his cheek. He turned and put his arm around her thighs. He turned back. "What's all this?"

"This is a research code Vandevelde uses. I've had to learn it, working with him. I don't know all of it. Look, here." She pointed to "X43b/s." "That means x-rays of the brushstrokes on painting forty-three. Or that 'att.' before the book reference means 'attribution.' Well, don't you think it strange these should be here—now?"

Sheridan was looking through the sheets. "Not necessarily. This," he said, pointing, "for instance. What do you make of this?"

"That's a reference to a standard work on historical oil paint compositions. But that—'redo. see w @ redh.'

I don't know. See someone in some book or article, maybe?"

"Yes." Sheridan flipped a few more pages, stopping to look once or twice. Then he pushed them away, smiling. "Very exciting, I'm sure. But if you want my advice, darling, I'd say, 'Do nothing.' I'd guess all this can be explained. Maybe they're the attributions Bobo consulted on for Horvay. After all, he was, is, the great authority. Look, if the police had any reason to be suspicious, they'd question him. . . . They're not exactly a shy lot."

She kissed his cheek. "Good. I'm glad I heard it from you. You know, an objective view sometimes helps. Only . . . if Karen asked me to, well, to snoop, and if it's her husband behind her . . . No, that's nothing definite either. Thanks, you're right, my sexy, sensible lover."

"I'll tell you what," he said with the tone of someone proposing a consolation. "You can write out those symbols you know, and I can try feeding them in with the other things I've toyed with on the computer. Not that it's turned up anything much for you, I'm afraid." He held the sheets of paper in his hand.

"Oh, would you? Thanks."

They went to sleep. Sheridan found himself walking in a museum. Long, long empty corridors, empty galleries. Shiny marble. He pulled himself towards the wall. A small painting. A windmill and an old red house by a canal. The windmill began turning in the wind. He jumped into the canal. The water came up waist-high so that he had to lift his rifle up. The wind blew the tops of the palms. A woman and baby sat looking at him. Like throwing a match, how they'd burn like straw. The water was burning.

Sheridan opened his eyes, sat up soaked with sweat. Where was he? Not where he could be calmed. It was all right. If need be. If he had to, he could kill them all. He looked at Georgia sleeping.

~~~~~~~ 5

Schwartz thought it would be bigger, like one of the smaller galleries in the museum. But once in the back-stairs corridors, he saw that the Office of the Chairman of the Department of European Paintings could barely hold the title, had it been spelled.

"And I'm impressed. The space really is saved for the public—like me," Schwartz said to Gerald Vandevelde.

"Oh, yes. Even the president's and director's offices are small," Vandevelde said. "The only treats back here are the paintings we get to hang on our walls."

Schwartz looked over Vandevelde's elegant salt-and-pepper hair to a painting. "Copies of the real things, right?"

"No. These are originals, Mr. . . . ah, Detective . . ."

"Schwartz, sir." He didn't bother explaining the title.

"Yes. Detective Schwartz. They're not even always our second best but for a variety of reasons aren't on current public display. But I'm afraid I'm wasting your time. Would you mind if I brought in our curator and administrator? Anything to do with this office concerns her, too," Vandevelde added with his smooth smile.

"Well," Schwartz began, trying to get the tone just right between thick cop and smart-ass, "this isn't office business, if you get me. But no, I wouldn't mind— terribly. You want someone else present? You got it."

He felt he'd overplayed it, made himself a bit grotesque. Maybe not. Vandevelde's smile was fading as he buzzed the intercom.

"Georgia Morris, Mr. . . . Detective Schwartz."

"Len Schwartz. Sure, yes, we met a few minutes ago in your . . . Nice to meet you," he said, shaking hands. She looked nothing like Angela Sylvester, but she made Schwartz think of her. "Well, sit down, relax. OK? Just a few questions here. Really to Mr. Vandevelde, but feel free to ask, you know, whatever." He sat and turned back to Vandevelde. "I guess you know this case, this Alex Horvay business . . ." Schwartz said, letting it drop to nowhere.

"Certainly. I wonder you're here only now. I would have thought you'd want to question me earlier. You or another senior officer."

"Oh? Why?"

A second of incomprehension passed over Vandevelde's face, Schwartz thought, as if he had wondered

205

if Schwartz was really dumb or had cleverly put him into a defensive stance.

"Obviously because he was a friend, a valuable consultant to this department, and because I had been professionally involved with his business, inasmuch as I was occasionally a consultant."

"And what did you . . . Oh, by the way, I'm not taping this or anything, in case you wondered. So what did you consult with him about?" Schwartz thought the "taping" a subtle touch of crudeness.

"A range of things. Sometimes the physical state of a painting or questions of history or style, iconography. That sort of thing." Vandevelde folded his hands on the desk before him.

"Many museum people are consultants to firms and individual collectors," Georgia said pleasantly.

Schwartz turned. "What?"

"I said that many museum curators are consultants, like Mr. Vandevelde."

"Oh," said Schwartz, as if not listening. He put his hand in his pocket, fished out a pen and small notebook and studied a blank page for some time. It was going terribly. Good. "So, let me get this straight. You say Horvay would ask you to tell him if a painting was real or fake, right?"

Vandevelde laughed. "No, I didn't say that. Sometimes the question of identification comes up, came up, in regard to style or physical state, but that hasn't anything to do with fakes. That is, not necessarily."

"Jesus, Mr. Vandevelde, you're losing me," Schwartz said.

Georgia said, "That just means a painting thought

to be by X may turn out to be by Y. Y may be a contemporary of X—better, worse, less known, but the now accurately identified painting is still genuine."

"Thank you, Georgia," said Vandevelde.

Schwartz nodded. "Right. Now I get it. Thank you—Georgia." He winked at her.

She looked at him and then at Vandevelde, and then both of them looked at Schwartz, with looks that said, "We're giving you our time because we're forced to, you dreadful little man, but we can't be forced to approve."

"So you're saying Horvay never gave you fakes to look at or that—"

"No. That is not what I've said. You seem to have some difficulty in hearing what I've said, Detective."

"Call me Len."

"As a matter of fact, Horvay did give me some fakes to look at."

Schwartz looked at Georgia; Georgia looked at Vandevelde.

Vandevelde looked straight at Schwartz and said, "Three or four over the twenty years I knew him. Three of them I remember he thought were fakes, too. But he'd been fairly sold on the fourth. It wasn't bad either. Technically not bad. But not for the eye. After a month I knew."

"So you told him not to buy it?"

"Alas, he'd already bought it. I told him he'd lost a great deal of money. It's all on record somewhere. Even the newspapers. Early seventies sometime. Well, we all like to think we can't be fooled, but sometimes . . . but I've gone on too long."

"No," said Schwartz. "No. That's very interesting. But you—you've never been fooled. Is that right?" Schwartz asked, jotting in his notebook, jotting tic-tac-toe.

"Several times. But not, to my knowledge, when it's made much difference. I was young; my opinion was overridden. I tried to learn from my mistakes."

I'm sure you did," Schwartz said. Then, abruptly: "Look, Georgia, I think maybe you should leave the room. I have some private business here."

Georgia looked to Vandevelde, who smiled and nodded. She left without a word.

"Just before you start, Detective. If I'm going to be accused of anything, I'll want to notify my lawyers—before answering. You understand."

"Oh, sure. No. Nothing like that. This is just an informal visit. Gerry, can I call you Gerry? Just trying to understand the sort of things Horvay . . ." Schwartz stopped and said, "You know I've been in Holland. Hurt my shoulder. Still hurts." He moved it. "Shitting awful pain, y'know, Gerry?" He thought he saw Vandevelde wince.

"Ah, you were there. I know of it. Not just from newspapers but from Baron Wartena, an old friend. It was his farm—"

"Yes, yes." Schwartz waved him quiet. "Listen, Gerry, you're really being very cooperative. I couldn't—you couldn't be accused of anything. I just want to set you at ease on that. No way we have a case," he went on, wondering what to say or do next. Something came to him.

Schwartz stood up and started pacing the small room

before Vandevelde's desk. He reached around his pocket absent-mindedly as if searching for a cigarette. He had none. He pulled his gun out of his holster and held it loosely as he continued to pace.

"I'll tell you, Gerry, before this case I thought I was a pretty smart guy. Not just a smart cop, you understand, but a smart guy. But this case . . ." He spun around to the door, went over to it and listened for eavesdroppers. Then he came back and leaned over the desk and, tapping with the gun butt for emphasis, said in a stage whisper, "This case—it's driving me bananas! Y'know what I mean? I feel like a dope, a real schmuck. Get me?"

He leaned forward more, rested one hand on the gun and put the other around Vandevelde's shoulder, saying, near his ear, "I can't make fucking heads from tails on this case. Off the record, I'm half afraid I'm going to lose my patience, my *professional* patience, see, and shoot someone's fucking brains out." Schwartz stood back again. "Off the record, of course."

Vandevelde was ash gray. "Detective, I'm busy. I'm sure you are, too. If you have no further business, I'd appre—"

"Right, right. Thanks for your help, Gerr. Oh, by the way, it's not 'Detective.' "

"Very well," said Vandevelde, drawing in a breath. "Len."

"It's Inspector Schwartz," he said. He put the gun back in the shoulder holster as he went to the door.

He opened it. Georgia Morris was at her desk in the next room. Schwartz turned back. "Mr. Vandevelde, I wanted to tell you how much I like that landscape.

Troost, isn't it? About 1740?" He shut the door on Vandevelde and walked past the staring woman. "Good afternoon, Ms. Morris."

And then he suddenly remembered that it wasn't football, that John Sheridan's sport at Harvard had been rowing.

6

Tom Gallagher said: "What kind of burlesque act did you put on up there? I'm getting phone calls all morning from the borough president's office, from some jerk at the mayor's office, a jerk, but from the mayor's office. And from Bill Farley, who may only be the *ex*-governor of the state but still has a bit of clout. Say, enough to have both of us directing traffic on Staten Island! Not to mention John M. Collins. You remember John M. Collins, Lenny? The commissioner of police. He was not amused. A soft-spoken man, but I know that pissed-off, quiet tone of his. And not knowing what the hell went off up there, I'm sitting here defending you, which is to say, defending both our asses, all morning. Don't interrupt!"

Tom Gallagher said, "Now, what they're telling me is that you did some routine up there—a combination of Clint Eastwood and Henny Youngman. You're spinning; you're turning; you're cracking one-liners, jumping up on desks, waving your gun under this guy's nose, poking it at paintings. You do that? Don't answer!"

Tom Gallagher said: "This, as you always tell me, is the modern police force, Lenny. The high-technology, educated new police force. What do you say—upwardly mobile. The goddamned Perrier police force. We don't send cigar-chomping mick gorillas or pushy Jew comedians for sensitive interviews in murder cases. Anyhow, just where the hell do you think you were, on the Lower East Side scaring the shit out of some spic dope dealers? Shuddup and listen!"

Tom Gallagher said: "Now, personally, I can take that art stuff or leave it, no disrespect for your lovely wife, Lenny. But the Met's the Met. It's the biggest single tourist attraction in this city. Not that I lose sleep over tourists. But they bring in lots of money and the city likes them and the city gives the Met lots of money and—listen closely and learn—it's very vi-si-ble. The Met is very visible! Get it? And I don't just mean up in the Eighties on Fifth Avenue. Personally I'll take the Mets over the Met any day, but they don't come from all over the world to watch the ballgame. They go to that place part run by that guy you scared the piss out of yesterday. And who's this guy? Just keep quiet and I'll tell you."

Tom Gallagher said: "This is a guy so well connected that when he sneezes in New York, the pope says, 'Gesundheit,' in Rome. This is the kind of person who when he was a baby had one of them baby-carriage nurses who was better born than you and me. Now get me straight. I don't give a flying fart for that Social Register crowd—but I respect power. You gotta; it's the world. And they've got it. And you know why they've got it? You're the goddamned intellectual sociologist, and you don't know shit! They've got it because they got here first and took it all, and took the money and kept it and bought everything and make so much more money. Jesus, they own the goddamned world. . . . And if they don't have it themselves, they've married it or their cousin has. And they stick together, just like the rest of us. So here's this, what's his name, Vande-face, who is very, very rich and is married to a wife who is very, very richer, and he knows everyone and belongs to all the clubs and, Jesus! you're swinging from his chandeliers and pissing on his head! You know what I think of that? Well, do you? Don't just sit there. Answer me!"

"What do you think, Tom?"

"Jesus, Lenny, it sounds terrific! I wish I could have seen it," said Tom Gallagher.

~~~~~~ **7**

Johnnie really was a brick. Busy as he was, when he'd heard the dismay in her voice, he told her to come right over. And he'd held her and fussed over her, sat her down on the sofa and brought a long gin and tonic, which Georgia had held to her forehead before drinking.

He was turned towards her on the sofa, stroking her ankles. She described the incredible visit of his detective friend.

"Hardly a friend, darling," he'd interjected.

"Whatever he is, after seeing him in action, I'm ashamed of any snooping I've done for Karen. And Bobo was so good through it all. I would have . . . thrown a chair at that animal. It wasn't even direct accusation. It was . . . slimy innuendo. God! How can someone like Karen live with him?"

"Who knows? Perhaps he's a hot Hebrew lover. Perhaps . . . he seemed ordinary enough when I saw them in Brooklyn. For that, they seemed an ordinary couple."

"Well, Bobo Vandevelde has one extremely chastened, extremely loyal colleague in me now. He just can't be involved in all that sleaziness."

"No, you're right, darling. Of course he isn't. You know all that data, those lists, everything? I programmed them all right. Absolutely nothing came of it. No, I don't know what my acquaintance Schwartz was up to, but I wouldn't think he'd try that again. Bobo's very well connected; he needn't put up with cheap police harassment."

"Is Schwartz anything in the police?"

"Yes, pretty high up. But even if he were commissioner . . . Oh, and besides, there was something a few years ago, some bribe investigation . . ."

"I'm not surprised."

"He was cleared, but it's paralyzed his career. Maybe he needs this case to get back on their promotion track. Who knows? He's done well enough for a little Jewish boy in a decidedly non-Jewish line. But of course, he's nowhere that Bobo's friends can't take him down."

Georgia smiled. "I think you'd make a terrific detective. Really."

"Perhaps. But I'd hate to work with that undisciplined scum."

She wanted to say that it couldn't be much different from working with his troops in Vietnam, but she didn't. He'd asked her not to talk about it, please. Her poor hero. "So," she said instead, "do you think I should call Karen? And what should I tell Bobo?"

"Don't bother to call her. I think her husband will have pulled her back. Besides, she'd assume that you wouldn't be interested, not now. Or at least wait until she contacts you to tell her. And with Bobo, too. Just be supportive. Don't bother bringing it up. From what you tell me, the poor fellow has enough to contend with without feeling he's the subject of his friends' pitying talk. You know how sensitive he is."

Sheridan's hands massaged her ankles and up from her ankles to her calves and the back of her knees. Georgia put the glass down and stretched.

"I do feel better," she said, "after talking to you. You're a good friend, Johnnie Sheridan."

"I'll show you how good, and you'll feel even better," he said, massaging her ankles and up from her ankles to her calves and the back of her knees and up.

8

It amused Sheridan, but he was in control; that is, the amusement was exciting, but he was in control. That Schwartz should corroborate his own conclusions—now that was rich. And as for Bobo, did it really surprise him? No. . . . He of all people could understand that Vandevelde, despite appearances—because of appearances—could have reason for more money. It was logical that Bobo made it through his professional expertise, just as if one were a trained soldier. . . . Still, it was a huge and rather enjoyable irony that he'd made the contracts. Of course, he'd never say anything to Bobo, never bring it up. Wouldn't particularly deny it. Everything was merely circumstantial. Very neat. Even had there been more, they'd have been safe, as gentlemen, with each other. Such a thing as loyalty. Families had known each other.

Just as once, twice, up in the highlands or into the Mekong you'd make contact with another special group, make out beneath the camouflage someone from Groton or your club at Harvard. And know you were right fighting those virus scum, right, even to the sack of heads you had, he had with him, too.

Sheridan watched his fist open and close as if he were squeezing an exercise ball. He stopped it.

Then there was the money. Oh, yes, you needed that. Well, you'd earned it, you'd made it, you'd invested it, you'd made back what your family had lost for the past two generations in this Jew's world. And now it was over. Really and truly independent again. Your own man. Except the one little matter of your "pal" Schwartz. Pushy kike. But no idiot. He'd bluffed Bobo into panic. Even that was no real evidence. But that was Bobo, who hadn't expected it. Who wasn't, in those ways, tough. No. Schwartz had nothing but was dangerous because of having nothing. Was probably just a bit mad.

His fists opened and closed, alternating in front of him. It was exciting, but he was in control. He stopped it. He laid the fingers of his hands together, held them up and pressed. Nothing. Schwartz had nothing on him. He'd tease him some more when they met. They weren't running. Oh, of course, his shoulder. Poor Jewish boy. Yes, they'd meet in that ridiculous "Gym and Racquet Club." Racquet Club, as if the Jew cop could get in *there*.

But that wife of his. Beautiful bitch, that black-haired Jewess. He'd like to get her tied down on his bed, chain-whip her and fuck her, like to rip her up in front of the little tied-up hubby yid, the blubbering yid.

His muscles tensed through his fingers up the back of his forearms into his shoulders and down through his pectorals.

No, she wasn't Jewish. That's right. Worse, she lived with one.

Simple in the delta. If you thought she lived with one, you let your men have her and you let them split her up the middle afterwards like a yellow melon.

His back and stomach muscles tightened and the muscles in his thighs bulged hard and his calves expanded as he pushed his hands together and his feet down hard. He was in control. He breathed in deeply and let go. He turned the power off. The light came to a dot on the console and went out. Now, what to wear?

"Sorry not being able to run," Schwartz said, getting up from the low couch as Sheridan came out of the rain. "I can do leg exercise, but it still hurts like hell to bounce it around all that time in a run." He touched his shoulder and held out his hand.

"That's all right. How are you, Len? You look pretty good for someone who—when were you wounded?"

"About six weeks ago now. Listen, excuse this place, but I had to be in midtown today and someone gave me a three-month trial membership here, so I thought, Why not? Here. I'll sign you in. My guest." Schwartz backed off, looking at Sheridan.

"Oh, this? My trusty yellow running suit, hood and all. It's waterproof, terrific for running in the rain."

"Looks light, too. Easy to pack. I guess you could take that anywhere."

"You can. I do."

"Wish I'd had something like that in Holland. It wouldn't have stopped the bullet, but I sure would have been drier. You ever been in Holland, John?"

"Oh, yes, several times. Lovely place. Amsterdam, those canals, the windmills, tulips. Did you get a chance to see much?"

"Too much and not enough. You know. Been there recently?"

"Yes. Let's see, about a year, a year and a half ago. Yes, about then. I'd have to check my passport."

"Yeah. Well, let's change," Schwartz said, walking ahead.

Sheridan followed, smiling, knowing Schwartz knew the passport check would be useless. He'd make the little fellow squirm.

He followed through a tight corridor. Mirrors to make it seem larger. Two fat Jewish women squeezed past in pink Yves Saint Laurent. Sweat gear made never to sweat in. The place was so awful.

Schwartz opened the door to the men's changing room. "Awful, isn't it, how they squeeze everything in? They must make a bundle."

Sheridan sniffed. The musk of a cheap cologne didn't mask the sweat and bitter foot smell; it mixed into a double stink. An old man was bending over, his shorts dropping from his crepe-skinned hips. The right half of his body trembled. Stroke. He turned around and smiled at him. Disgusting. Great Jew liver lips, the sagging, shaky body and the sex, the heavy balls and big . . . Sheridan looked away. Yes, best put out of their misery.

"So where's your gym, John? Don't tell me you don't work with weights with a body like that?"

Lord, was he homosexual, too? "A place not unlike this," he said, "because it's convenient to my apartment. Up on Lexington. But then there's the AC."

"The New York Athletic Club?"

"Yes. It's a nice place. Do you know it?"

"Of it, of course. You know the joke, don't you?"

"What joke?" Sheridan looked over and saw the deep red crease running from Schwartz's armpit up into his shoulder.

"About Cohen meeting Finkelstein after years and the two of them bragging about who's done better, has more houses, cars, like that. And finally, Cohen says, 'So, *nu,* you've got everytink, my friend, and still dey von't let you in.' 'Let me in vere?' asks Finkelstein. 'The New York AC, dey're not letting you in.' So one thing leads to another, they get angry, and it ends with Finkelstein betting Cohen half a million dollars that he can get into the club within ten years. Cohen not only takes the bet, but gives him three to one odds.

"So first Finkelstein changes his name to Rogers. Six months later he changes his name to Whitney so that when people look at that face and ask him what was his name before it was Whitney, he can say, 'Rogers.' Then he does everything. He moves from Larchmont to Old Greenwich, joins the Presbyterian Church, sends his kids to Hotchkiss and St. Paul's, donates a quarter million for the improvement of the country club, and for five straight years takes lessons in a foreign language—WASP.

"Finally, he's ready. He gets one of his new buddies

to put him up for membership in the New York AC. No sweat, he's voted through; there's nothing left before he's a full member and gets Cohen's million and a half but a little interview with the membership chairman. No problem, his buddy tells him. Just relax and be yourself.

"So it's the interview and Finkelstein is nervous, but by God, he's going to put it over on these people. And the man is very nice, doesn't ask him trick questions. 'Sit down, sit down, Mr. Whitney,' he says, 'I'm Hammy Pierce.' 'Please, uh, call me Chub,' says Finkelstein. And the man's looking over the membership application and saying how they're looking forward to having him a member and that he sees Chub's son, young Christopher, is at Hotchkiss—so is his and maybe they could go up to parents' weekend together. And he sometimes plays at the country club—they could make up a foursome. And Finkelstein is saying, 'Sure, sure,' to all this and he's getting more and more relieved and relaxed. He can see he's in the New York AC. And the guy shakes his hand and Finkelstein realizes he's done it! And he shakes hands, and as he's leaving the room, he turns and says, 'Oh, by the way, Hammy, though you didn't ask—it's all right, I'm a goy.' "

"A goy?" Sheridan pretended. "I don't quite . . ."

"Uh, that's Jewish, Yiddish for 'Christian.' You see—"

"Oh, yes. I get it. Quite good," he said, lacing his sneaker. That should hold Mr. Schwartz for a bit.

The gym, as Sheridan expected, turned out to be designed for people over seventy-five who'd had major heart surgery. And who were dwarfs. He said this to Schwartz, who nodded, laughed and said, "Look around. That's who's here, except me and you, and with this shoulder I feel more like them."

Schwartz put himself onto a bicycle machine. Sheridan went to the weights machines and adjusted it to do squats. For a while they worked away quietly. Some old people left the room, talking loudly, complimenting each other on the exercise.

"I suppose," Schwartz said, "you heard of the mess I made of it with Vandevelde."

Sheridan let it ride. He squatted and straightened. Squatted and straightened. Kiddy weights. He stopped to put them all on. Did Schwartz know he was friends with Vandevelde? Yes. Georgia, probably. He squatted and pushed up. Better, now, something to push against.

"Yes, I heard something about it from Georgia Morris. I see her."

"Yeah, I know; that's what I figured. Jesus, these aren't as much fun as real bicycles. Not that you don't get anywhere. I'm used to that. But you don't see anything on the way. To nowhere."

"Since you bring it up, Len, yes. I hear he was shocked. He can't really be a suspect, can he?" said Sheridan, lifting up, looking at Schwartz.

Schwartz pedaled. Then he said, looking straight down into the pedometer, "Hope you're not offended, John. I mean, I don't know if you're close friends or what, but I'm rather afraid that, yes, he's a suspect."

Schwartz pedaled. "Suspect, hell, the fucker did it. I don't think I'm gonna get him, mind you, but the fucker did it all right, sure as my shoulder's hurting on this stupid machine."

This was really too interesting. "I don't know how the police work, Len, but are you saying that Gerald Vandevelde shot someone in cold blood?" Sheridan asked, adjusting his speech to his breathing.

Schwartz pedaled. "No. Murdered, not shot. And no. I'm not saying he did it."

Schwartz pedaled. Then he started to laugh, pedaling. "Come on, now, John. You know I don't think Vandevelde would soil those elegant white hands of his. He bought the contract. You knew I meant that. You're kidding around with me."

Schwartz pedaled and laughed.

Sheridan squatted and lifted. He wouldn't let the little sheeny get to him. He was in control.

"Anyhow," Schwartz continued after a while, "what's the difference? No way of getting through Vandevelde's lawyers, his rich wife's rich lawyers to trace the money, painting by faked painting. Or for those contracts on Horvay and the Dutchman."

Sheridan stopped, stepped out of the frame and wiped the sweat off his forehead. "Dutchman? The Nazi the newspapers said hanged himself?"

"The very one. But hell, I'm a cop. I'd know how to hang him so it'd look like suicide. Hell, you were a Green Beret major, right? So hell, you'd know how to do it, too. Not everybody would. But hell, it could be done. And the Nazi bit—yeah, I buy that's who he was. But I figure that was a kind of blackmail or an insurance policy that was cashed in. Yup, quite a setup. Enough. I'm tired of getting nowhere."

Schwartz stopped pedaling, dismounted and rubbed his shoulder.

"Interesting," Sheridan said, moving towards Schwartz, "but isn't it . . . ah, rather . . ."

"Circumstantial? You bet, John. That's what I'm saying. Between heavy lawyers, heavy influence and no hard evidence, I ain't got shit. Except maybe the actual killer. Now, here's the real irony. In the whole deal I figure he's the most innocent in a way."

"A paid killer, a Mafia-style hit man most innocent? You're a curious policeman, my friend," Sheridan said, looking at Schwartz's shoulder.

"Why curious? Why Mafia, for Christ's sake? Shit, I'm not J. Edgar Hoover, but I don't think they do *all* the killing. No. This guy's innocent in the way that all loonies are."

"You think the killer's insane? Ah, I see. A moral judgment."

"No, no, John. Jesus, I'm not expressing myself well. Sorry. No, I'm saying there's some hard evidence here. This killer is a real fruit cake—you know, pounds and *pounds* of almonds and angelica in there," Schwartz said, tapping lightly on the side of Sheridan's head.

Sheridan put his hand up to Schwartz's scar. "Six weeks? It's coming along very well, Len. Sign of a healthy body." His thumb went into the scar groove.

Schwartz jumped.

"That hurt, Len? A very good sign. Almost no nerve damage. Take it from an old soldier. You'll be all right if you take care." He smiled down into Schwartz's sweating face.

"Thanks, good to hear it. No, as I was saying, John,

the evidence. That little schnook in the middle. The one in the green track suit, you remember, the one dumped on the Hans Andersen statue. Some sort of delivery boy, I guess. Now that was the act of a madman. See, that wasn't a contract. That was pure fun. Fun! Listen, sooner or later this crazy bastard *has* to show himself. Has to—how can I put it, John?—has to *dare* to. Know what I mean?"

Sheridan smiled. "I do. Yes, I do."

"Hey, that reminds me," Schwartz said, pointing to a rowing machine, "your sport at Harvard wasn't football; it was rowing."

"Yes, rowing. I didn't say—"

"Didn't you? Football? Didn't you say football in Brooklyn? My mistake then. Jesus, that seems years ago. Karen still asks after you. She thought you were the best-looking thing since Gary Cooper. I keep telling her she means Alice Cooper, but she says no. So, do you still row? Weren't you some sort of star in those little ones, one-man things, you know . . . ?"

"Sculls, single sculls. Yes, I keep it up. It's fine all-round exercise. Up at the top of Manhattan, near Baker Field."

"Oh, yeah. Nice. I was up there once in the summer. Lost in time. Right out of Eakins, the kids diving off the rocks. This city's like that, the best places too scruffy for development. They stay more natural, wilder, something. Yes, I remember you were some rower. Went to the Henley Regatta in England, wasn't it, our senior year?"

"Yes, the Diamond Sculls."

"Jesus. And all I did was place in the Penn Relays

and I thought it was pretty good. My dad hoped it wouldn't make me turn pro. Can you imagine that? Fourth in the Penn Relays? He was crazier that I was." Schwartz began waist rotations, grunting as he rolled the wounded shoulder.

"You getting physiotherapy for that, Len?"

"Yeah. But I do better exercising myself," he said, rolling up, side and around, grunting twice in each rotation.

"If you wanted, perhaps I could help. I learned massage techniques out East. Some of them were developed along with acupuncture."

He said it casually enough. They were the only ones left in the little gym.

Schwartz stopped his rotations. "Sure, John, I take any help I can get." He said it in a crazy voice, staring, raising his big eyebrows up and down like Groucho Marx.

Schwartz took off his sleeveless sweat shirt and lay face down on an exercise bench. Sheridan placed his hands on both sides of Schwartz's neck and pulled away, down the tendons, back to the neck and around, pressing on the small vertebrae. Then he repeated it, each time working out closer to the shoulders.

"Damn," said Schwartz, "whatever you're doing, it's terrific. You should bottle it. Ten times better than the physio."

"Well, hard exercise helps. Your blood's already flowing fast; your muscle temperature is up."

"Well, you have magic hands, no doubt about it. Really relaxing. I could fall asleep."

"Yes, the idea is to relax, open up the circulation,

227

breathe slowly and deep," said Sheridan, his fingers working in, pulling softly from what would seem inside. "How is it on the shoulder?"

"Good. Stiff, a bit painful, but very good. You must have been a godsend to your troops."

"Not the word I'd use, 'godsend.' Sometimes it was helpful when we couldn't get the morphine or whatever. Mostly it was beyond all that. All they wanted was . . . simple enough, but I couldn't give it to them." He went on in the steady massage rhythm, pulling, kneading, pulling, kneading.

"What?" Schwartz asked.

"One bullet to end the suffering. That was the humane thing in the situation."

"I see. And you never . . ." Schwartz's voice dropped delicately.

"Officially, no. You understand. You think it was immoral?"

"God, no. Who am I to judge?" Schwartz's voice came slowly. "I think it had to be a very moral choice, really, either way. Jesus, what a choice. No one should have to make it."

"You mean that, do you, about its being moral?"

"Of course."

"Thanks." Sheridan was pressing around, over and between the neck vertebrae with gentle, heavy pressure. "But I disagree about not having to make it. Those choices always have to be made. Most people can't handle it, aren't equipped to make those hard choices. Politics, it seems to me, should be such to insure that those who can are in the positions where those choices have to be made."

Schwartz's voice came slowly. "Oh. And who are those people?"

"Perhaps I'm old-fashioned, but I think they're people who've been born and bred to choose and to live by the moral implication of those choices."

"Choose. You mean 'rule,' don't you?" asked Schwartz in a dozy drawl.

"Hmm, yes. I'll tell you who they weren't; they weren't the jackass generals, senators and fat theoreticians running us in Vietnam. What a farce. Had we sent them into the jungle for a few months they'd have known what to do. The few who survived, I mean."

Schwartz's voice came from a sleepy distance. "What—what would they have done, John?"

Sheridan's fingers moved deep into the shoulder. He slid his hands back. His fingers covered the back of Schwartz's neck, pressing in over the top of the vertebrae and into the side. "I'll tell you a story to answer that. A true story. It even had some celebrity back then; at least, it got around Nam. It seems there was a horse called Johnson's horse. Not for LBJ. Maybe the first person to find him or care for him. Anyhow, a rarity, a fine horse in Vietnam. No one knew where he'd come from—a plantation, a descendant of some French horses. But there he was, a beautiful white stallion up in the forests of the northwest DMZ, near Cambodia. Johnson's horse. He became the special mascot of the units up there. They cared for him, cleaned, curried him, stole the best for him. And nobody rode him. The horse was a legend. We'd all heard about him.

"The troops dreamed of him—a symbol, you see.

229

Strong, graceful, free. All that. I thought so, too, at first, before I'd been in there, in that wet jungle that was killing us, putting its wet, soft mold into our hearts. Well, a year or so later—by this time my little outfit had some reputation, too—a year later we actually meet up with the unit up there looking after Johnson's horse. And they make a big deal of it, one of those shifting, high-casualty cavalry units curious to see what old pros like us were about. So the commander. . . . Are you awake, Len?"

"Mmm."

"A captain—a serious, twitching West Pointer—doesn't bring the horse right out. No, first, there's a dinner and party laid on in our honor. They want to know this, that and everything about us. We keep pretty quiet. Friendly but quiet. Then this captain tells the story of Johnson's horse, makes the animal sound more wonderful than Pegasus.

"Finally, it's led out for my inspection. There it is. Johnson's horse. A fine white stallion in the jungle clearing, in the moonlight. The firelight. I stood and looked into its big black-brown eyes. A wonderful horse. It pawed the ground. I blew into its nostrils. It stood still. I killed it with a shot between its eyes. It reared, fell back and rolled to the side and down quite dead. Are you awake, Len?"

No sound from Schwartz but the deep breathing.

"And in the shock and silence I told them *that's* what our unit was about; *that's* what the war was about if we wanted to win. It wasn't about playing farmhand nursemaid to a horse that did no work. I left it at that. I didn't bother telling them that I'd also done it for them and for the VC watching us from out there, or, of course, from in there mixed in as dear old ARVN fighting with the cavalry. Let Giap and Ho see there were some of us who understood. Only there weren't enough."

Suddenly Schwartz's neck rolled from under his hands, and Schwartz was sitting up. "Don't tell me— then you had them chop the horse into hamburger and fed it to your troops?"

"What? How! You li—" Sheridan's fists closed tight. He took a deep breath. It was all right. He was in control. "I thought you were asleep."

"No, you're good with those hands, but I used the shoulder pain to stay awake."

"What do you mean?"

Schwartz stood up and started shifting from foot to foot. "You know, about how we both, for instance, could put someone to sleep and then string him up. No, only kidding. No, of course, I wanted to hear the whole story. I'm glad I did. That was some story. You are one crazy fucking man, you know that?" Schwartz said, smiling so that he could be understood as complimentary.

Sheridan would take it that way. "Len, I think that neither of us is what you'd call average."

Schwartz was dancing around on his toes, bobbing. "And what a massage! Terrific. Look at how loose I am. Well, the right can't do much. But it's there."

Sheridan smiled, in control. "Some open-hand boxing, Len? I'll be careful of your shoulder."

Schwartz danced around. He threw a few jabs. "Why not? No one around now. But just open hand. And take it easy. You're twice my size, and you have all that reach over me."

Sheridan kept smiling, moving in. Schwartz was jerking about like a badly worked puppet. This would be fun. Sheridan said, "I promise to take care."

He jabbed over Schwartz's guard onto his right shoulder. This would be fun.

"Ouch, shit," said Schwartz, dancing away. "Good thing that was just open hand, anyway." He grinned. "Lay off the shoulder, please."

Again Sheridan kept a long left jab leading out. Schwartz couldn't get near him with his silly, dancing gait. This time, when Sheridan picked off the shoulder, he poked stiff fingers in.

"Oh, no, really," Schwartz said, wincing, "that's enough."

Schwartz came forward.

Sheridan sensed the change in Schwartz just before he understood it. Schwartz's left jab went open-handed but straight-fingered into the bottom of his ribs. Sheridan swung at nothing. Schwartz's left hook swept into Sheridan's right eye; his head seemed to hang just at the end of Sheridan's right fist without the fist being able to connect.

"Naughty, naughty. No fists, now. Remember, John?"

Sheridan felt his face stung, spun around, his nose slapped up hard and slapped up hard again, and all he could touch was Schwartz's right forearm and back. Enough. Boxing wasn't his thing. Time for karate. Why not?

"Hey! Hey! None of that here, please. Find a gym

with a boxing ring if you have to," said the attendant, passing through with a stack of towels.

They'd stopped.

Sheridan found his T-shirt spotted with blood. He wiped his nose. Blood was smeared across the back of his hand.

"Hey, John. Jesus. Lie down here. Yeah, just put your head back. Here, I have some Kleenex somewhere here. Just a bloody nose. Sorry about that. Here, just stuff a bit of this right up."

"You box. I didn't remember you boxed. You set me up," he said, trying to smile. He couldn't.

Schwartz was bending over him, smiling. "And I didn't remember you rowed, killer."

Sheridan held the Kleenex to his nose. "Killer?"

"Yeah, an old boxing nickname. Boy, we were really going. Just as well we didn't have guns. We would have lost control, huh?"

"Speak for yourself."

"Oh, I was, killer, I was," said Schwartz with the big grin and the sweat that was dropping onto Sheridan's face.

Sheridan breathed deep. Very well, very well. So he wanted to play rough. Very well. It was all right. He was in control. What fun it would be to play rough with the Jewboy's pretty wife.

9

Karen wasn't surprised. She hadn't been expecting to hear from him, but when John Sheridan's voice came over the phone, it seemed the natural continuation of their first meeting. Months ago? Days ago, it might have been. And she'd reacted like that, as if she hadn't thought of him or seen him, vague-featured figure but absolutely him, night and daydream.

Yes, of course, she remembered. Did he want to speak to Len? She had Len's office number. No, he wanted to speak to her actually.

Yes? How could she be of help? It concerned that business Georgia was helping her with, the art matter. He'd come up with something.

But why hadn't Georgia . . . ? Ah, no, something which . . . Well, he'd rather not talk about it over the phone. Might it be possible for her to see it herself?

He needed her professional opinion. Today, lunch-time, though he knew it was inconsiderate notice. But it did seem urgent to him.

All right, but it would take some time to be ready and then get over to Manhattan. That was all right because he would be downtown and would pop over the bridge and pick her up. No, he was sure it would be no trouble, and he very much looked forward to it.

Karen washed, did her hair and chose her clothes with a care that made her smile. She knew what she was doing. No, not really. Len wouldn't be using her in this . . . No, that was silly. She was silly. She could call back. Where? Not be here when he came? Why? Frightened? Yes and excited. Her mother's expression "There's no hell, but if there was . . ."

Len had told her to stop looking, stop contact with Georgia. But nothing about Georgia coming to her. Well, John Sheridan. Such rationalizing! So.

She called Len. Len wasn't in. She left a message. Seeing Mr. Sheridan. She'd call. She'd take care.

She was watching out the window when the Bentley stopped. He got out. Years before, she'd had a two-week affair. The only infidelity in her marriage. Why was she thinking of it now? As if she didn't know . . .

She went to the door.

10

At two in the afternoon Gallagher said, "You're right. He doesn't seem the kind of guy to complain about how you treated him."

Schwartz nodded. "More the kind just to kill me for it, quietly."

"Right again. If he's your man. Now, if he kills you, Lenny, you know you got the whole weight of the department behind you."

"Behind my corpse. Well, yes, but in my last few warm-blooded hours, what?"

"Respect, Lenny. Profound respect. Look, I'm crazy letting you go bait these guys like you do. And what do we have on Sheridan? That he starts screwing Vandevelde's assistant after Horvay's murder? That he's got an army shrink record which fits, which fits probably fifty thousand guys, including Martin Bor-

mann? That physically he could have done everything?
Yup. And that adds up to the froth on a glass of piss.
We couldn't hold him ten minutes if we pulled him in.
OK, so I agree this calls for something special, the
great Lenny Schwartz creative flair. And your man
makes a move—bang! you get everything we've got.
All official then."

"Tom, how come you're so nice to me?"

A line buzzed on Gallagher's desk. He put it on
hold. "You know what I'm going to do? I'm gonna
assume you're not taking the mickey out of me and
give you a straight answer you probably don't deserve.
Upstairs," Gallagher said, pointing straight up with a
big index finger, "they've finally gotten pissed off with
all these subtle hints from the hundred and twelve
most powerful people in the city to lay off this one.
They want to show them the department's not totally
twisted."

Schwartz tapped the desk. He stood and leaned
across to Gallagher. "That answer is so twisted . . .
that I believe it."

Gallagher was on the phone. "Yeah? Yeah," and
gave it to Schwartz.

"With who? When? That's all? OK, Bob. I'll get
back. Get me if there's another call from her."

Schwartz handed it back to Gallagher. "Jesus, I'm
so stupid. I didn't think. Listen, that was a message
from Karen. She's gone out with Sheridan; he said he
had something personal for her on the case. Jesus! So
now it's official."

There was a long pause. "Lenny—" Gallagher began softly.

"You prick," said Schwartz flatly.

"Oh, yeah? You telling me you didn't sort of half plan this?"

Schwartz ran out of the room. Gallagher was right. If they pounced now, Sheridan'd do nothing. But fuck it, he had not wanted to use Karen for bait. Oh, yeah? He ran through headquarters, muttering, "Prick, prick, what a prick I am."

~~~~~~~~ **11**

When Karen got into the Bentley at noon, she knew she'd made a great mistake. Something in the way the door clicked when it closed—quiet, final. She'd wanted to flirt, and this handsome, handsome man beside her, polite, smiling, had her feeling like she had as a teen-ager when she'd found herself on a date with a wild driver.

Sheridan drove slowly and well. Karen tried to think of an excuse—some appointment she'd say she had to get to. It was so simple. All she had to do was say it.

She couldn't find anything to say. He kept driving, a pleasant expression on his face. Approaching the Manhattan Bridge, he turned the car off to the left. Karen started to ask where he was going just as he started to tell her. They laughed.

"No, please," she said.

"I thought it would be nice over the Brooklyn Bridge. It's such a fine day, and we can swing right onto the FDR uptown. Should we have the top down?"

"Yes."

They pulled over. When the top was down, Karen felt better. Sunshine, wind, the other cars. They were so visible now. What infantile panic! Enough.

"Well, what's the big mystery, John? And why tell me and not Len?" She heard her businesslike voice.

They curved left onto the bridge. The tires whined; cables gleamed above them, swung up higher into the ship's rigging through which the sky poured down; lower Manhattan buildings soared.

"Wonderful, isn't it? Different each time, this lovely old bridge." He smiled at her. "No mystery, Karen. I thought some delicacy might save bad feelings here. I'm terribly sorry if you thought . . . It's that you're friendly with Georgia. And if you thought . . . I'm not saying this very clearly. Let me begin again."

Karen felt much better now. He was human, someone who was having trouble saying something.

"If you think what I've found should be shown to Len, fine. I'll call him right away. But if it's nothing, well, this way I'd be able to keep Georgia from being interviewed. And, well. I'd rather. . . . Oh, dear."

"It's all right," Karen said, not able to keep from smiling. "I know Len can sometimes carry on. His 'style.' " She laughed.

They passed into the shadow of the central pier. Had John been blushing? She couldn't tell now. He was nice. His light brown hair flew in the wind. His fingers on the wheel were long and elegant. Stop it, she told herself. Well, if it's only in my head, it's all right, she contradicted. She stretched against the soft leather and ran her hand back through her hair.

Coming onto the FDR Drive, Sheridan said there were some photostats, but it would be clearer seeing them, to compare them.

Karen said, "Yes," not really listening, looking up to the end of the island where the water shot high into the air. "Look," she said, "the Delacorte. It must be the first time this spring." The water shot straight up white, then plumed, spraying away into fine rainbow mists the winds blew.

He said, "In honor of the weather."

She saw him look at her. She knew she looked pretty. She felt pretty. Still, he wasn't flirting, hadn't said "in honor of our drive" or anything like that. She closed her eyes to the warm sunlight, opened them in the shadow of the underpass, closed them again when they came out into the sunlight off the drive. It would be nice in the Met. Why the Met? What he'd said about Georgia . . . She opened her eyes. They were headed up First Avenue. They could be going to the Met. No, it didn't make sense.

"We're not going to the Met?"

"No." He shook his head, looking ahead at the moving, swerving traffic. "We couldn't very well go there. The material's at my place."

At the next light he turned to her. "Oh, Karen, of course, if you'd rather. Oh, of course. I'll run up and get it. Not the same as on the video display, with the other figures, but of course . . ." He was beginning to stammer.

Cars honked. He turned and drove again.

"No, that's . . . of course, that's all right. But I can't stay long." She was embarrassed. How could she simply have said no? Insulting. What was she playing at? She could have said no by saying no, and that was that. Well. She'd called Len anyway. And she'd call him from John's apartment.

They turned off at Eighty-eighth, went up a few blocks and turned in on the curb before the double doors of an old stone and brick stable. John got out, opened the doors and drove the car into the large garage. A few other cars and a pickup truck were lost among its shadows. He opened the door for her.

"I'm surprised this hasn't been converted into condos, like everything else that stands still in New York," Karen said.

"In a way I suppose it has. I'm upstairs."

He shut the doors, and they went into a large elevator, not quite passenger, not quite freight. Everything worked with keys.

"This used to be the mews house for our family place across the street. That went years ago, torn down. This was all that was left. So I've kept it and converted it."

"Were you brought up across the street then?"

"No. They lost . . . it went before I was born. Here we are."

He unlocked the door. It slid open. "One tries to hold on to whatever's left, whatever they don't destroy."

Karen drew her breath in. God, what he'd held on

to! "It's unexpected. I mean, how still, how large, deep." She laughed. "I think I mean that I love New York because the strangest and best, like this, is so often hidden away."

Sheridan smiled and nodded to a half bow. "That, coming from the great art historian, is a compliment."

They were in a small entrance hall, a near-perfect cube of about twelve feet. Its other side opened to an enormous living room, where light streamed in through skylights and the three windows she saw, moving forward, floor-to-ceiling windows at the far end, the part built three stairs up.

His hands touched her shoulder as he took her coat. She walked in quickly and looked at paintings, books and old Delft.

"Would you like a drink?"

"What do you do, John? If I may ask, I mean. This—"

"I'm a private investor, Karen. A pretty serious one, a pretty good one. Not a rich playboy. Aside from the building and a few bits of furniture, I've worked for all of this. Now, some white wine?"

"Yes, thanks. I haven't offended you, have I?"

He turned back and gave her the . . . well, damn it, it was just the most beautiful smile she'd ever seen on a grown man. Then he came closer and she saw his eyes. And they were beautiful and cold. Something in there was too steady, too . . . locked.

"No, of course, you haven't. I'm to be excused really. But all the assumptions about 'my sort.'" He laughed. "I'll get wine. Please look around, make yourself comfortable."

Karen looked around. She couldn't make herself comfortable. She felt excited and afraid. This place . . . She looked down into a hallway. Light, open doors . . . but . . . She found herself tapping a wall. Almost no sound. Yes. That was it. This place was like a well-lit vault.

"Does it pass the building inspection?" he asked from across the room, tray with wine and glasses shining in his hands.

"Oh, yes. With room to spare." She crossed and went up the stairs and sat at an armchair by a small table at a side window. She took the glass he poured, sitting in the chair opposite.

"A small toast," he said. "I propose—the truth. Not honesty, that everyday mask over the truth. The truth."

Karen looked at him, a small question turning up her lips. For a wild second she thought of drugs in the drink. No. "The truth," she said, drinking. The wine was wonderful, a great white Burgundy that rubbed her tongue. She saw him standing naked in her bathroom, the gold-brown hair on his hard stomach she imagined like the wine on her tongue. "I like the wine."

"Good," he said.

They looked at each other.

"So, having proposed the truth, I propose telling you the truth. I *do* have those photostats to show you, but—"

"But that's the 'honesty' part of it?" Karen put in, quickly looking down at her glass.

"Yes. The truth has more to do with your black eyelashes and your hair against your white skin."

Karen looked up. "That's my mother's side of the family, the black Irish from the west, the ones who took in the remnants of the wrecked Spanish Armada. So they say."

"Is it true?"

"Who knows? But it's honest. I think that's all I can manage."

They drank wine.

"I want to make love to you, Karen. I want to take off your clothes and kiss your throat and all the rest of you," he said slowly, his voice dropping softer at the end.

Karen watched her hands lift the glass to her mouth. That wine, his wine. "I'm flattered, I think. Why me? There's Georgia, there's"—she looked across, smiling—"everyone else, even prettier, the very beautiful."

"You're very beautiful."

"You're right, the truth is harder than honesty."

"Very well. It will sound strange. You excite me because your husband suspects me of murdering Alex Horvay."

Karen felt her face flush. Stupid thing to do, blush. She was frightened but forced herself to look at him. She thought that her fear might be more than either of them could bear.

Now he was looking down into his glass. "And that's why I excite you," he said quietly.

She couldn't stop. "No, that's why you frighten me. Did you kill Alex Horvay?"

He looked at her with steady blue eyes. "No, I didn't." He smiled. "But that's not the point. It's that your husband believes I did, wants, needs to believe I did. That's exciting, isn't it?''

"Perhaps exciting only to someone who did or could have killed Horvay."

"Oh, Karen, *anyone* could have killed an Alex Horvay. No, your excitement has as much to do with you and your husband as with me. Someone like you, a policeman's wife, however clever a policeman. I see you, Karen. And I've read your book. So perhaps I see your excitement as you can't."

Karen felt the wine in her head; her body lightened. Her glass was full again. All right. Why not? "Perhaps I can see yours that way, too, John. Perhaps it excites you to think of making love to Len—through me."

She hardly believed what she saw in his face: not a twitch or tic but some agony starting somewhere within those eyes, moving in a wave through the muscles of his face, down through his cheeks and mouth, up into his forehead, rippling back into his temples. No, it had to be the wine.

"Really," he said in a light-hearted voice, "I thought women had pretty much dismissed the theories of that turn-of-the-century patriarch Jew of Vienna."

"Say, reevaluated. And Jews have nothing to teach Christians about patriarchy."

"Ah, touché. Excuse me, Karen. All I can do in apology is offer lunch. Yes?"

She nodded. It gave her some time. Nonsense, Karen. She fussed with herself. He's wonderful-looking, and some food would be good and sobering.

The dining room was small and delicious and orange-pink, like the salmon they ate. Sheridan poured from the second bottle of Montrachet. The wine circled around the glasses, the talk around their excitement. At one point they agreed that it was as if Len were there, the third person at lunch. At another, Sheridan described his "wild game" hunts for his Claude and Poussin and the Delacroix. At other points she kept coming back to his homoerotic feelings. It angered him, she saw, and she couldn't quite decide whether the anger was a safeguard or a danger. But it excited her, this talk mixing Len and John. And she was talking with John and Len wasn't here, so that in some mad way it was Len who had become the fantasy figure. In other words, talking of John's love for Len was like making love to both of them at once. Then he saw how it excited her and wasn't angry.

She looked at herself in the bathroom mirror. She washed her face with cold water. She looked good. She saw that somehow Sheridan and Len were connected. When she straightened her dress, her hands passed over her breasts. Something cold moved in her womb, up to her eyes. She looked in the mirror. Of course, Len was right. She was flirting with a killer. This place. She'd just go.

He stood in the hall, framed in the light from the living room.

"I have to go now, John," she said, but didn't believe.

He drew her into his arms, his hand up her dress in her underpants.

"No, stop it."

"Shh. Shh."

She tried to shout no. Incredible, how he could just

247

scoop her up like this, so her mouth was muffled against him as he carried her.

It was his hand on the back of her neck that pulled her head into his cashmere jacket, his hard chest. She felt that. But less and less as he set her on the bed . . . his fingers on her neck. So slow. She felt hands soften against him. Then the light dimmed; the vault door shut.

~~~~~~~~~ **12**

She wanted to fly. She was a bird chained down. She started flying, but the wing chains were pulling her down into the buildings, down past empty windows. She fell through the glass skylight. The glass cut.

She opened her eyes. She couldn't see. Her face was pushed down. She was face down on his bed. She pulled. Her arms and legs were tied down.

The sound came, and she felt the pain across her buttocks like glass cutting the flesh. She wanted to sleep, to stop being, but she couldn't stop. The slight deep pain at the back of her neck where he'd put her to sleep.

She was naked, pillows under her stomach. Screaming was no good. The chains were real. The dream, real. Light chains, locked bracelets she felt, wrists and ankles. Where was he? She turned her head to the side. Light on the sheet. How could she save her life? That was it, wasn't it? White linen. Raped on real linen. Or it was not rape. What did it matter if he'd kill her? Where was he? Too quiet. A shadow across the corner of her eye. The sound again . . . the cuts. He was whipping her.

She'd have to say what? Crazy. He'd kill her? No, don't think of that. She'd have to pretend she liked it. No, don't think of that.

What? She felt his hands run lightly up the inside of her legs, spreading them. She pulled back, but the chains, his hands too strong. His hair on her thighs. She clenched; he wouldn't. But he pulled and his tongue was in her ass. Let him whip her again so she could think. This was too . . . Something she should say to . . . His tongue was in her. Out. Where was he? Gone.

Shadow. Whip? No. His weight in back of her arms. She saw his ankle now. He was over her the other way. Pulling them open. Licking her ass, opening, licking her down her vulva, and his hands pulled her clitoris down and up and out and his tongue . . .

How could she kill him? Not to feel good like this. What to say that would kill him? Too good, the feeling. Stop thinking that. The pain. Oh, God, that pain was just right. If she enjoyed it, he wouldn't kill her. No, he'd kill her slower. No, if he killed her, he'd enjoy it. Say something.

She wanted to open her legs more. No, she didn't, wouldn't. She couldn't love him. God, not come, she was going to come. Not that. Say—

"He knows I'm with you. I called Len before. He knows," from the corner of her mouth. Good. Stopped him. His ankle went. The weight lifted.

The whip cut down on her again. Again, again. God, good, good, let him, good, past pleasure this pain past pleasure into thinking how to kill him. Karen cried with relief at feeling the pain.

"No, you didn't. He wouldn't have let you see me."

Wanted, she wanted to say she'd left a message. She stopped. That wasn't it. Wasn't how. How?

He was undoing the bracelets on her ankles. She put her legs together.

"Now I'm going to let your arms free and you're going to turn over and not try anything silly like running away. It would only hurt you. Oh, yes, and you're going to smile because you enjoy this. Understand?"

"Yes." Oh, good God, that saved her, that "and you're going to smile." Smile? She'd laugh in his face, the stupid, spoiled, fucked-up brat. She didn't know how, but it saved her.

"Good. You're very beautiful," he said, unlocking the wrist bracelets.

He was standing by the bed, naked. She thought of a terra-cotta figurine she'd seen. Pre-Hellenic. Cycladic? What was she thinking? The figurine, too, has that big prick sticking. If he put it in her mouth, she'd bite it off. Let him kill her. What's he doing, standing there waiting for me to applaud? The fucker. Where was Len?

Sheridan knelt on the edge of the bed. He touched

her breast. His index finger was moist around her nipple. He was, he was. She lay still. Good God, if he wasn't a crazy killer, she'd have been his lover. She would not feel guilty. Those fuckers, those men, all of them. They wouldn't make her feel guilty on top of all this. On the bottom of all this. It made her smile. Where was Len?

Sheridan lay down by her side. Len, too. All of them were crazy. Len was. Len was as crazy as he was. Yes.

Sheridan's face was over hers when she said it: "Bait."

His hand moved over her belly. "What?" he asked quietly.

"Bait," she said, "I'm bait. You're through. He can't get you any other way, so he's setting you up with me."

Sheridan smiled. "Not even a good try, beautiful. I can't go to jail for adultery."

"Not jail. He's crazy. You know that. He's going to kill you. Just shoot you. Bang. You know it."

"No, no. Why would you tell me? Why, for that matter, would you let yourself be used—if the rest of your silliness were so?" he asked, his voice still quiet, but seeming less amused.

"Because," she said, stalling, "don't you see? I don't.
. . . I didn't even know. I just figured it out. The whole thing," and Karen started to cry. God, she felt it could be true. She hated that crazy bastard. Len. John.

Sheridan picked her chin up in his hand and looked at her.

"He's . . . John, he's crazy. For all I know he could be, I don't know, getting off on this. He, oh, God, he could be up there right now watching through the skylight."

Sheridan's hand shot out around her throat so that two fingers pressed deep in. She couldn't move.

"He's not up there," he said, letting go.

She stopped crying. Her heart pounded. Had he seen anything, a shadow, he'd have killed her just like that. But Len could have been up there. She wouldn't think of it. She wouldn't go to pieces that way.

"Get dressed."

She looked at him. His prick was down. She'd done that much. She'd get dressed. What else?

"Karen," he said quite seriously, "thank you very much for the warning. I don't mind taking my chances with Len. I'll be ready now."

Was he right? The crazy egomaniac really thought she was warning him. . . . Had she? What had she done?

"Well, we should probably leave here. But we won't run anywhere. Don't worry, my pretty one. No. I know, let's go . . . to the Met. What a perfect way to end the afternoon. No, we'll meet whatever we meet—directly. Even Len. Especially old Len. Perhaps we'll tell him about us, darling. Perhaps not. Whatever you feel best. Now let's get ready. I'll be a few minutes. Just stay in here and the bathroom until I return. You really are very beautiful."

He went out and shut the bedroom door.

She washed her face. She looked in the mirror. She

was all right. She'd saved her life. For now. She brushed her hair. Her hands shook. Don't think of that. Who was at risk now? All three. Three? How could she still think of that crazy killer? Which crazy killer? She caught her smile in the mirror. Someone was going to die. Not her. She hoped it wouldn't be Len—just.

13

Schwartz and Bob Malinowski were standing by one of the flower vases in the great hall when Karen and Sheridan came into the Met. Schwartz said something quickly to Bob and went towards them, smiling. He kissed Karen.

"You all right?"

"Yes."

"Hello, John. Jesus, I'm glad my hunch was right. I've been looking everywhere for you—two," Schwartz said, in a loud, flat voice, one of his flattest.

"Hello, Len. What's up?"

"What's up? Will you listen to the guy? I was scared for Karen. Let's get out of here."

Small angles appeared on Sheridan's face, but he kept his voice pleasant, saying, "Now, please, no silliness. We've had lunch and now Karen's going to give me the expert tour of Monet and Cézanne upstairs."

"Silly?" said Schwartz, putting his arm around Karen. "My wife running around town with the toughest hit man on two continents and I'm silly to be worried? Let's talk about this outside."

Some passers-by stopped and looked at them.

"Hit . . . man." Sheridan repeated the words slowly as if mouthing something strange that turns out unpleasant. "Len, or is it Inspector Schwartz? If you plan to arrest me, do it now or please stop your insults. I won't be played with like this, and I have no intention of going outside with you. I came to the museum with Karen. And here we'll stay."

"OK," said Schwartz, walking towards the admission booth by the stairs, his arm tensing around Karen. He turned. "Come on, John, if you're coming. Let's see the pretty pictures. You know I have no plans to arrest you."

Sheridan's eyes narrowed. They relaxed, and he followed them. "My treat," he said.

"Wouldn't hear of it. Pay for yourself," Schwartz said.

Some people in line looked away; some looked at them and smiled with embarrassment until Sheridan's eye caught them, and then they looked away, too.

Karen showed a card and got a button. Schwartz showed his badge and got a button. Sheridan's patron card was half out when he changed his mind, paid four dollars and got a button.

Karen smiled at Schwartz, kissed him and whispered, "He's armed."

"Thanks for the kiss, darling," said Schwartz.

They went up the grand staircase together, Karen between the two men.

Schwartz knew he couldn't move. Bad shoulder or not, Sheridan on his worst day could kill him, and Karen, while he was still fumbling with the stupid gun under his armpit. Just keep riding him, he figured. See what happened. Get the whole force on his ass and keep mine—and hers—whole.

"Hey, killer, you know what I can't figure is what you're going to do when the word goes out that you're just another nut, you know, like those Jersey greasers. What are you going to say to all your pals at the Union Club and New York AC?"

"Len, you're an idiot. Don't you think he's an idiot, Karen?"

"Yes," she said, looking at Sheridan, "but then I always think Len's an idiot. He always thinks I'm an idiot, and we're always proving each other wrong."

"Like Karen going out with you," said Schwartz, speaking straight ahead and quieter. "Or like that," he continued as they reached the top of the stairs and he pointed towards the huge bright Tiepolo. "I never see figures in his work, just terrific abstract painting. I mean, Jackson Pollock has nothing on that guy."

Karen smiled. "I don't think that's idiotic." She touched Sheridan's sleeve. "You don't think that's idiotic, do you, John?"

Sheridan backed off a step and smiled. He looked at the Tiepolo, then back at both of them. "Not at all. I think it's very clever. I think you're two very clever people. Shall we go on."

"I think," said Schwartz conspiratorially, "we're *three* very clever people. And that's not even counting the split personalities, Major Sheridan." He winked and slapped Sheridan lightly on the back.

Then, in a Yiddish accent, he said, "Say, det's a good piece material you got from your sport coat. Kemel? Kishmere?"

Sheridan walked off towards the Tiepolo Room.

"OK, John, sorry," Schwartz called after him. "I know how you detest *that.*"

People were looking at the loudmouth. A guard came towards him; Schwartz showed the badge and waved him off.

Karen ran to John and tugged him back to Schwartz. "Come on, John, Len. Stop fighting, boys. Be nice. Can't you be clever *and* nice? I can." Karen linked arms with both men. "I know," she said, "let's not look at old Impressionists or old Cézanne, though I love them dearly and they help pay the bills."

Sheridan said, "And don't forget the drug bribes."

Karen smiled sweetly. "Now come on, be nice. You promised. Let's—let's go around the balcony to the Chinese section."

"Is that to see here or to take away?" asked Schwartz.

Karen laughed. Sheridan didn't. Schwartz came around to Sheridan's other side as they passed the poster shop.

He leaned in towards Sheridan and whispered, "Personally I'm glad we didn't see those paintings. I don't think I could take all those nude women."

Sheridan looked straight ahead.

"Jesus. Degas alone, they got room after room of

those naked women bending over. No, sir, I'm in no mood to look at . . . Hey, you like that stuff? You like taking them from the rear, John? In the rear? Women, I mean. Women in the rear of the museum?"

Sheridan looked straight ahead. Schwartz looked over to Karen. Karen looked straight ahead. Her cheeks were flushed. They passed cases of Chinese vases.

Schwartz looked straight ahead. He spoke louder. "No, I envy that gay bachelor life of yours. Oh, *gay* in the strictly old-fashioned sense of the word, naturally."

Sheridan's cheekbones stood out, but he looked straight ahead. They came onto the balcony.

"Except," continued Schwartz, "the killing part of it. I don't envy that. Especially the way you do it. Little bits of nose bone in the brain. Yech! Call me a sentimental fool, John, but those Mafia hit men seem all-American boys compared to you. What happened, they get you over there in Nam? You a Commie or something?"

Schwartz had his back against the balustrade, his arm out along it. Karen had dropped off back at a display case. Sheridan stood in front of him, looking up at the light through the top of the dome.

"Len," he said quietly, "do you know how easy it would be for me to throw you over? Have you any idea what a thirty-five-foot fall onto stone would do to you?"

Schwartz looked around and over. "Hmm. Probably wouldn't be much fun for anyone I fell on either. Well, here's a tip for you. See, there, where Karen's looking? Those turquoise jars? Anyone tries to sell you that color turquoise as old, say, Ming or earlier, be careful. Probably fake. Most of that color was made much later, made for the Arab trade. So if your pal Bobo Vandevelde comes around one day with a suitcase full—"

"My dear Jewish friend, you can't touch me," Sheridan whispered. "Your sort never could, never will."

Schwartz nodded. *"Also Sprach Zarathustra,* and look what happened to him: died of toothache in Uruguay."

Schwartz came away from the balustrade and passed Sheridan, saying, "And speaking of supermen, will you look at this one?"

Karen joined them at the plinth of the statue.

"Of course," she said, "it's magnificent, the Canova. But the subject is so . . . well, sexist. Isn't it?"

Sheridan asked, "Perseus with the head of Medusa?"

"Oh, sure," Schwartz said, "any dope, male dope even, knows that. I mean, there he is. He's cut the head off. And of course, the Medusa isn't a monster. I mean symbolically it's what man fears." He was speaking loudly again. "You know, John, what he fears— the female, the old cunt, as a matter of fact. Isn't that right, darling?" he asked Karen, putting an arm around her.

"So," he went on, "he's only safe, in the political psyche he's created, with her completely tamed—that is, dead. Classic craziness. Karen, you wouldn't know this, of course, but my friend John has a body about as wonderful as Perseus here."

Schwartz maneuvered Karen behind him.

Sheridan said, "Len, I believe I'm thinking of hitting a police officer."

A wave went through the muscles of his face.

"No," said Schwartz, "I don't think so, old man. You see, if you hit me, I'll try to kill you. I wouldn't, of course. You'd kill me. But then, you see, every cop in New York would be after your lovely *tuchis*. A kind of loyalty there, old man. And you are good. But not against the entire police force. Not even you, my old *übermensch*.

"This, John"—he nodded at the statue holding out the severed head—"is the kind of stuff you're good at."

Sheridan stood very still. He turned and started walking away, along the balcony.

Schwartz pushed Karen back, turned and whispered, "Get down behind the plinth."

Then he called to Sheridan in his very ugliest, loud, flat voice. "Come on, John, don't be a spoilsport. Don't be a quitter. Hey! I know. Let's go say hello to your pal Bobo. Lots of laughs that. Me introducing the contract maker to the hit man."

Sheridan kept walking. It wasn't working. Schwartz kept waving people away with his badge wallet.

"Hey, John!" he shouted. "Then we could—Georgia, too—talk about the best places in the Met to fuck—"

Schwartz fell to one knee, turning sideways as Sheridan spun. Something hit the back of his neck. People turned. Someone screamed. A man yelled, "Watch it!" Screams, then, and Sheridan took off.

Karen was OK. Schwartz took out the radio. "OK, Bob, call in, he's moved. Shot at me. Say very, very dangerous. His car." Schwartz looked to Karen. "Yeah, the public garage. Only armed security. No, Jesus.

Careful, he'll kill sixty visitors. No, tell their security not to try. We'll get him ourselves. Call!"

Karen was putting a handkerchief to his neck. "It's a bit off the statue, I think. Just a scratch. I saw it fly off the Medusa. Good thing you weren't looking at her."

~~~~~ **14**

Bob sat beside him talking into the radio and rubbing his bruised knee as Schwartz turned the car onto Fifth Avenue. Sheridan's house was covered, the avenues and crosspark streets around the Met were covered and the helicopters were informed. And New York traffic wasn't exactly jammed with brown Bentley convertibles.

On the other hand, Bob and two armed guards had been waiting for Sheridan down in the Met garage and he'd gotten away. Bob said "flying out of nowhere" onto the two guards and then spilling Bob to the ground when he'd run up to help. Using nothing but his hands. One of the guards would definitely be all right. Bob had got off lightly.

"Don't fret, Bob," Schwartz said, cutting over to go down Park Avenue. "No one could've done more,

263

considering. And get off the line. They'll spot his car any second."

"Sir, why are we moving like ordinary traffic? Why are we going this way?"

"I don't know. What's the use of rushing? And where are we supposed to go? His house is covered, and Georgia Morris's and even the Met, still. So I thought we'd head downtown. Jesus, can't they spot a goddamned Bentley? Have we gone crazy with the equal hiring policy, are we using blind drivers and pilots? OK. Let's get nowhere faster. Lights, sounds, action!"

The lights spun, the siren whined and Schwartz took off towards the Pan Am Building. At Fifty-ninth, when he had to slow from sixty miles an hour to ten while a panicked florist tried to pull his van back to the curb, Schwartz noticed Bob's hands gripping white-knuckled on both knees.

"Relax, partner."

Bob turned and grinned, turned back and stopped grinning as Schwartz gunned the car. Bob was pretty good; Schwartz pretended not to hear his muffled "Please" as they rounded the right angles of the Grand Central ramp doing thirty-five.

Then Gallagher came on for him, and he slowed and asked what the hell was happening, where was the famous full weight of the force, had the force gone on a crash diet or what? Gallagher said they'd put everything into the Upper East Side first. Now they were getting mid and downtown vehicles into it and the choppers would be over the drives in minutes. And did the inspector approve and would he please stay in touch?

Bob looked at Schwartz.

"Yeah, he's right. He's doing it all right. So pay attention. He's a good, careful cop. We're after a panicked master killer, who's also very smart and who just might have a howitzer in his Bentley. Or bombs, for when he turns it into an airplane. So all we can do is not panic."

"I'm not panicked, sir."

"OK. You're relaxed and I'm driving beautifully. So let's go on downtown. Maybe John wants a ferry ride."

He drove with the flow of traffic down to Union Square. Nothing. Nothing on the radio. Was the Bentley in a garage? Had he gone on foot, hired another car?

"Bob, are car rentals covered?"

"In Manhattan, yes. Description's going out."

"Good. A longshot, but good."

They had just come onto the Bowery when it came through. The helicopter spotted the Bentley heading south on the East River Drive, just passing East Houston.

"Jesus, it's close!" said Schwartz. "Put everything on again, Bob."

Schwartz had the car up to fifty. Here came Houston. He slowed to forty. There was another siren sound just before the crash. The car spun, hit nothing, swung as in slow motion and crashed into the other police car.

Schwartz sat there thinking that the good news was that everyone was OK. The bad news was that he was obviously an actor in some sort of Keystone comedy.

"What the fuck!" screamed the other cop, opening Schwartz's door.

"Yes. Well put, Sergeant. My car no longer works. I see yours does. I'm taking yours. You and your partner will take care of traffic around this wreck. Come, Bob."

There. For once he was showing Bob some sensible behavior.

Horns blew and a crowd formed. Two winos emerged and began washing the window of the wreck before the Sergeant could say, "Yes, sir," puce-faced, to Schwartz.

They moved off in the other car. The Bentley was turning off into Grand Street.

"Bob, I think he's tired of Manhattan. So am I. Let's go quietly, no lights."

Schwartz turned the car onto Delancey Street. The front tire screeched in the crumpled fender. He yanked it back.

"I think I see him. Look down there," Bob said.

"Where? Yeah, yeah, that's him. About six blocks of pretty slow, steady traffic. What do you think, Bob?"

"Me? Oh, yes, sir. I could, no, my knee. Well, you could go on foot and . . . whoa!"

Schwartz jerked the car. The right side of Delancey Street was closed off for repairs. It was empty. Emptyish.

"Hold on," Schwartz yelled as the car hit the broken, grinding surface. He knew it couldn't take too much of this, but they were making up one, two, three blocks.

"That man all right?"

Bob looked back at the fat man whose shoe they'd grazed. He was hopping. "Yes, sir. We're—"

"He's seen us. Put on the siren and lights."

The Bentley had pulled into the closed lane. It was moving fast. Stones, dust sprayed out behind it. Schwartz didn't dare go faster on this surface. The Bentley pulled back into traffic. Cars crashed; horns blew. The Bentley had made the right side of the Williamsburg Bridge.

Schwartz made it about a thousand yards behind. But Schwartz had the siren. Schwartz also had smoke fuming from his engine.

"We're gaining, sir."

"We're losing oil."

The Bentley drove wildly, beautifully, Schwartz noticed, finding himself thinking that was one more thing fucking Sheridan did well.

"You know what he's doing, Bob? He's riding our siren. Clever fellow. Your gun ready? Your vest on?"

"Yes, sir."

"What's in this car?"

Bob looked around. "Just a loud-hailer in the back seat, sir."

"Bring it up here. We can hail him to stop in the name of the law, and he'll die laughing. Another vest back there?"

"No, sir."

"OK. Take yours off. You'll stay by the radio. I'll do any running needed."

"But, sir, the helicopter's right above and—"

"Gimme that jacket. That's an order. Please, Bob, that'll help most," Schwartz added, thinking that nothing would help most. Well, a few divisions of commandos might. Anyhow, he wouldn't let Bob go down for a John Sheridan.

"He's coming off the bridge, sir."

The radio said the same, without the "sir."

"I see, I can see! Terrific, all this help I'm getting. The entire force describing what's happening to me! Hey! Do you see what I see?" Schwartz asked in real amazement.

"He's turning right."

"Yeah, Bob, he's turning right into Williamsburg. Why?"

The car was getting worse. The smoke was coming blacker and thicker. Schwartz made the end of the bridge and turned right onto Roebling. Hasidic kids in velvet yarmulkes were running, *payos* swinging, looking up, pointing to the burning police car.

Schwartz heard a crash. His car started bucking, stopping, jerking forward, stopping. Stopped.

"Stay at the radio till the others come. Tell them—"

Bob was already talking when Schwartz jumped out and started running with the loud-hailer in his hand, twisting, doing a little running dance to get the flak vest on.

Up there was the Bentley, at the corner of Lee Avenue. It was crashed into a truck, its long, elegant hood smashed through the side so that its ornament was lost under the sign MOISHE MEYEROWITZ. ORTHODOX WIGS. HI-FASHION.

The street was a mayhem of jumping children, women in bandannas bending over baby carriages and bearded men pointing up the street, for Schwartz.

"That way. A meshuggina! A shtarker! By there!"

Schwartz looked up Lee Avenue. Sheridan had left a wake of panic. Shopkeepers out, traffic stopped, horns blowing, an old, old Hasid rocking, praying.

He climbed the hood of a car to look. A backwards wake. The farther up he looked, the less there was to see. Of course, fading in and away. The old soldier. Schwartz put the loud-hailer to his mouth and pressed it on.

"This is the police, the police. Attention. A very dangerous man is here. Be careful. Very tall. Blue eyes. He's probably armed. He has a gun. Very dangerous."

Schwartz stopped.

Then he added, "Keep off the street. The man is dangerous. A terrible anti-Semite!"

Schwartz jumped down and trotted up the street. Baby carriages, little kids, women, old bearded/young bearded men. He was drenched with sweat under the flak vest, his jacket, shirt. It had become a hot summer late afternoon.

He wouldn't pull his gun out. Useless panic. Too many on the street. Schwartz kept trotting. Jewish bakery, religious goods, dry goods, signs in Yiddish, Hasidic schools, babies, women with bandannas and the old men, flowing beards, young men gaitered, Warsaw in the eighteenth century. And Sheridan of all people to fade into this?

Sirens coming up from Greenpoint. Yes. Exactly. Where were the other forty thousand cops? Or one other? It didn't matter. Schwartz slowed to a walk. Running didn't matter. Save your strength, he thought, and felt scared, felt he'd love just now to take a leak.

Yeshivas, kosher butchers and *glat* kosher, more kosher than kosher butchers, and still crowded but quieter here. Little boys with curly earlocks playing with tricycles. A few more blocks and he'd never find—

What was it? What was so strange about . . . ?

He turned back and stood before the dirty window. Lee Avenue Hasidic Tailor. Finest Quality. In the window a headless tailor's dummy with a black Hasidic long coat. Strange old-fashioned black-on-black patterned silk, standing in dust. He remembered Sheridan's ritzy English tailors. Very cute. No.

But . . . The door here two steps down. The sign CLOSED swinging a little. Anyone could close a shop anytime.

A small crowd behind him. He waved them away. He looked in. No one. Racks of long black coats, ritual vests. Lights on. He turned the door handle. Open. He took out his gun, set down the loud-hailer and pressed the flak vest closed. And went in.

What worried Schwartz was all the people out there, that and all the stillness in here. Racks and black racks, narrow passageway. He'd have heard the door. Schwartz crouched; he lay down on the floor and looked under the racks. Nothing, nothing. A closed door at the end of the passageway.

"Hello? Hello?" Schwartz called out. "Anybody here? Anybody back there?" The dust was up his nose.

A noise behind him. He spun, gun pointed. Oh, shit, no. A boy was pushing a baby carriage into the shop. Two babies!

"Get out, out," snarled Schwartz.

The boy looked curiously at Schwartz and smiled. Then he saw the gun. Then a woman was behind the boy, screaming in Yiddish and pulling him back. The boy fell backwards onto the steps. The woman went berserk trying to pull the fallen boy and the baby carriage back up the stairs. The babies started to wail.

Schwartz started laughing and got up. What a mess. "It's OK—" he began when a shadow passed across him and kicked his head and Sheridan landed at the carriage and in the same motion pushed it, knocking the screaming woman over onto the boy and knocking the carriage up and sideways and one baby fell out onto the woman and Sheridan smashed through the shouting crowd.

And Schwartz didn't dare shoot. He couldn't even get through the door. He picked up the loud-hailer and leaned over the carriage.

"Anti-Semite! He's armed!"

Schwartz twisted over the carriage, over the bodies, twisting, stumbling, watching. Screaming, shouting all over the street. Sheridan vaulted a car. Schwartz saw the flash of the gun in his hand. He didn't dare shoot.

He watched Sheridan across the street. An enormous bloody-aproned man appeared, stood before him with a raised fist. Sheridan's gun lashed up as the huge fist came down on it, like knocking away a fly, a wasp.

No gunshot, thank God. He saw Sheridan pause for a second, look at the giant butcher, black-bearded, yarmulked, then turn and run.

Schwartz crossed the street and saw Sheridan's gun at the giant's feet. He smiled up at him and started running after Sheridan.

It wasn't exactly his turf, but more his turf than Sheridan's. There he went, tall and easy to see.

Half a block off Lee, with people pointing "there,

there," it came to Schwartz that the odds were equal, Sheridan not so much running for his life as running against his, Schwartz's, against this part of town, against all these lives. Oh, and he had a gun. Sheridan didn't.

He heard the sirens back on Lee. Wonderful, just where he needed them. Yeah, the odds were just about even. There he went; he'd stick to more crowded places. OK, Schwartz, do something simple and brilliant.

Schwartz stopped and peed in a doorway.

He cut away from Sheridan and came into Broadway at Havemeyer much closer to him. A fat cop joined him at the Chemical Bank.

"Tell them not to get close . . . not to try anything near people. He'll kill anyone."

The fat cop nodded and stopped, out of breath.

Across Broadway, Havemeyer became a small, tight Latin barrio, where Sheridan's high head was easy to see. Some kids were jogging with him now, excited by the gun in his hand, the loud-hailer in his other, the sirens wailing around.

"Fuck off, amigos. That's a killer up there."

The perfectly wrong thing to say. The kids wouldn't fuck off. This was fun, running down the hill. One of them ran with a ghetto blaster, Latin music. "El Amor de Mi Corazón." Enough.

"Listen"—Schwartz stopped—"either he's gonna shoot you or I'm gonna fucking shoot you!"

The kids stopped running. He went on. One of them yelled, "We thought you was real, not a mother-fucker cop."

Sheridan came to the bottom and turned onto Metropolitan, deciding that two blocks behind was just fine, for now.

Under the Brooklyn-Queens Expressway Schwartz knew he'd lost him somehow. And where was anyone else? Why was he the only cop in the city?

He came out—an Italian area. A square, some benches. A few men sitting on . . . he saw it, but too late. The man across the square, sitting on a bench, taking a shot at him. The loud-hailer jerked back in his hand, flew out, busted. Blood on the back of his hand. Not his gun hand. OK, so the bastard had another gun. The bastard. OK. Enough.

"You're finished, Sheridan. Give up!" he shouted. He started running.

Sheridan was staying on Metropolitan Avenue, running past the clean clean ticky-tack of imitation siding stone and imitation siding brick and brick mixed with stone and imitation siding wood and past Don Bosco Council K of C and the wrought iron. And Sheridan, he knew, would give up about as fast as he'd become Hasidic, Puerto Rican, Italian, and, now, running out of crowds where Maspeth crossed Metropolitan, black and Spanish by the derelict wings of Greenpoint Hospital, the strangely neat park across from barbed wire and, now, fewer and fewer, a few lone houses of fortressed, boarded windows, and the factories began.

Where were the others? Right now, one goddamned squad car and they'd take him. Where were those lovely squad cars that pulled up by the dozens at those twenty-dollar break-ins?

Sheridan ran. Schwartz ran after Sheridan. The blocks were longer. The street smelled of glue and chemicals. Puddles, mud puddles he ran through. The odd, old tenement in a half acre of weed.

IGLESIA PENTECOSTAL. ARCA DE SALVACIÓN INC. Empty and unempty factories. Not Sheridan's part of town. Not his. Not, shouldn't be, anyone's. One-story factories, empty, unempty. Please, just one small squad car. Please!

Gas tanks. Open sky, empty. The streets. Old tracks. Gas tanks. They were running on the moon. They were running toward the gasworks?

The street changed before Schwartz, from dirty surreal to clean surreal. Clean surreal was scarier. Towers, tanks, pipelines. Schwartz and Sheridan, the only two humans left alive. Rust-mountain scrapyards away to the right. No helicopter but a sea gull wheeling overhead.

"Sheridan!" he yelled into the quiet.

Three hundred yards ahead Sheridan stopped, turned.

"I don't want to have to shoot you, but I will," Schwartz yelled, keeping running, but more slowly.

Two hundred and fifty yards now, maybe, the gun heavy in his hand. Slower but still closing. Sheridan standing there waiting for him to get into range. Shit.

He stopped, didn't dare get closer. Sirens from way back, from South Jersey probably.

"Listen," he shouted, "I'll shoot you. I don't like guns, but I'm good with them or lucky or something."

Sheridan standing still out there on the crazy nowhere street waiting to kill him.

"Will you please give yourself up?"

Sheridan's voice: "No, I think not."

"Please."

He saw Sheridan shake his head no. Schwartz raised the pistol as Sheridan turned. Schwartz aimed and fired once.

Sheridan kept running. What did he expect? Too far.

He looked at Sheridan moving away and realized where they were. He walked after Sheridan.

Schwartz walked. An orange butterfly so early? Red admiral, was it, flying through and through the green chain fence, from emptiness to emptiness, the empty street? The huge and strangely prim Brooklyn Union gasworks and a madman up ahead running towards the dead end of Newtown Creek.

Sirens off in back. Schwartz walked and looked at his hand and decided this somehow wasn't it. Sheridan, who knows? would fly away or have a fur-lined U-boat waiting for him or . . .

Between chain fencing, the end of Maspeth Avenue lifted in a mound of earth and gravel. Weeds and reeds and bushes sprang from the top. Sheridan disappeared over the top.

Schwartz crawled up. Sheridan could leap on him any second. Kill him any way he wanted, any way that turned him on, God damn it. Only by now Sheridan was probably in Newport or Biarritz or . . .

Schwartz pushed his head over the top.

He saw the gun first, at the water's edge. Then Sheridan on the big broken stones. His hands were at his throat.

Schwartz crawled up, stood up behind the gun he pointed down. Then he saw the blood all over Sheridan; then he saw the blood pulse through Sheridan's fingers, a small red spring.

He'd shot Sheridan through the neck and throat and jugular. Anyone else would have missed. He jumped down. Anyone else shot like that would have dropped right away. He knelt.

And almost fell back when Sheridan opened his eyes.

A tiny liquid gargle of a voice said, "Lucky Jew."

"Just a cop," Schwartz said. He put his mouth to Sheridan's ear. "Come on, now, John, you can tell me now. You killed them, didn't you? It was you. Just nod, don't talk."

Schwartz lifted his head and looked down. The worst smile Schwartz had ever dreamed came onto Sheridan's cold face. It stayed. His red hands fell away from his red neck. The dead blue eyes stayed open.

Here were the sirens.

"Down here," he said.

Then Gallagher's voice: "Lenny? You OK? Oh, shit. What a mess. Where the hell is this?"

"A canal," said Schwartz, "Newtown Creek. The stretch between—I'm not kidding, Tom—between English Kills down there and Dutch Kills up there."

~~~~~ 15

Finally, they'd had Ed and Ben over for dinner. Rather a grand dinner, as Ben said; grand with guilt, as Len didn't say.

Little lobster somethings that Karen made for starters and then Len's filet en croûte that all agreed was tons lighter than tired beef Wellington. And very fresh vegetables and salad and cheese and Karen's vacherin that everyone said should be marketed immediately.

And a lot of very good wine so that Ed had proposed they were celebrating Len's imminent promotion, to which Len wouldn't say yes or no but said it was to celebrate Ed's full return to health. And they tried not to notice how the once-fine features of his face were permanently thickened.

Ben suggested they were drinking so well and too much in honor of Karen's receiving the National Art

Book Award, to which Karen responded by thanking Ben and saying that they really should be celebrating the announced retirement of Gerald Vandevelde as chairman of the department of European Painting at the Met.

Then Ben said no, they should really really be celebrating Karen's being able to say all that without a mistake after so much wine. Then Ben said, what about him? He was the only one who hadn't been toasted and he pretended to cry, so everyone toasted him, and as they drank, he saw the flattened bridge of Ed's nose and really began crying, pretending to pretend.

Then there was coffee and brandy and Ben's rather wicked dissertation on two types of pretentious brandies and brandy servers—the VPs or vulgar pretentious, in the thick, twisted bottles with engraved labels poured from horrid wrought-iron coddlers and the EP, or elite pretentious, and here he looked at the bottle in Len's hand, in the elaborately nondescript bottle with the apparently handwritten labels. And just to show, he said, that he wasn't being bitchy, he'd admit he made a terrific profit from both kinds in his liquor store. Then Len toasted Ed and Ben, books and booze, the perfect couple.

Then Ed wanted to thank Len, seriously now, for being a friend in the police force to the gay community. Len shook his head, mumbled he'd done nothing and thought how true that was. He said they'd see when he was commissar of police or commissioner, and the others all said, yes, commissar, commissar,